CHRISTMAS in Wichita Falls

A SPECIAL HOLIDAY ROMANCE

CYNDI RAYE

Christmas In Wichita Falls

A Special Holiday Romance
for
Mail Order Brides of Wichita Falls
by
Cyndi Raye

Cover art by Black Widow Design

---

1. http://www.CyndiRaye.com

Dedicated to Rowdy

This old man was a loyal one. His heart was stout and his love,
fierce. He wore the name proudly and thus made us proud of him.
His heritage was that of a proud race of the finest Shepherds from
the Black Forest. A member of this family forever now may he rest
in peace alongside others fallen. It was a great joy to have this great
boy share time on this earth with us so let us not mourn but
rejoice in thunderous cheer that reverberates through the heavens.
R.I.P Rowdy
- Eulogy written by D.N.L

Chapter 1

"A what?"

"A Christmas Ball."

"That's just silly. What do you plan to do, have people dress up with those fancy masks to hide their faces?"

When there was nothing but silence he swung around. From the look on her face his eyes widened. "You are serious! Lily Sloan, you are going to host a show-stopping masked ball for the folks of Wichita Falls, aren't you?"

He stopped short of laughing in his cousin's face when her husband turned up out of the blue and swooped her up in one giant hug. Ben Sloan was madly in love with his wife, it was obvious to anyone who walked through the doors of the Wichita Falls Hotel, which they owned.

David Morgan turned away while the two exchanged a kiss. He didn't want to see people caring about each other. Not like that. There was a time when he thought he'd have a relationship like Lily and Ben had but not any more.

He was done with love. All he cared about was his work. David knew how to fix things. He was able to fix anything he touched. Like magic, he knew how to tear something apart and put it back together even better than before. His cousin called it a gift.

It wasn't a gift. It was hard work and common sense, was all. He'd be called upon all hours of the day to fix things that others were not able to. So, maybe he did have a gift if that's what you wanted to call it. To him, it wasn't a bad living. He had a small shop along main street, right across from the church where he would fix and repair most anything. Most of the time he'd be out and about because folks called him to their homes and farms.

His living quarters was a big two story house behind the shop. He didn't use the whole thing, a room or two at the most. The rest of the rooms were empty and they'd stay that way as far as he was concerned. He'd never get married. David's plans were to live his life simply by helping others while making an honest living. He turned back to the two love birds.

"David, you're staring." Lily giggled, snapping David out of his deep thoughts.

"I'm not staring, Lily. You should not be kissing in public like so."

"Why not? I'm a married woman. Perhaps you'd like to know my secret that I'm going to share Christmas Eve at the ball."

David chuckled. He loved her so much. She was always smiling, teasing and making others happy. She loved to entertain so it didn't really surprise him when she announced a holiday ball. He supposed he'd wind up helping with the lavish party.

Lily hadn't always been so filled with happiness. A long time ago, one of the rancher's in the area had held a secret over her head, causing her much grief. She had pushed away Ben so he didn't get hurt but in the end he became her hero and her husband. Ben had loved Lily since forever.

"Perhaps I'll ask Ben about this secret instead of you," David teased.

Ben flung his head back and laughed out loud. "I have no clue what she has in store but I sure can't wait to find out. Now, my Lily, I'm off to do some work. Would you like to come along."

Lily gushed. "I'm afraid I am busy with David. He's going to build me a stage for the Christmas Ball."

"I am?"

She nodded. "Yes, and I need help with the giant tree I spotted yesterday a few miles from here. Plus, we have to get invitations out and I've got a great idea how to get the invitations to our community. David, I'm afraid I'm going to need your services up until the Christmas Ball."

He sighed. "What you are looking for is an assistant and I'm not your personal assistant, Lily. Just because you are my cousin doesn't mean I can't refuse to be hired by you." Although, Lily paid well and up front. She never hesitated or offered him a chicken or services as replacement for cash like some of his customers had done.

Lily winked at David and turned to her disappearing husband. "Ben, darling? Can you write David a nice fat check so he doesn't run off on me? You know how important this Ball is."

Ben laughed out loud again. He shook his head. "What Lily wants, she always gets, David. You may as well get used to it."

"I'll take cash."

Lily swung around, her eyes wide when she realized her mistake. "I'm so sorry, David. I didn't mean for you to have to go into the bank. Although, sooner or later someone is going to pay you with a check and you will have to face the music."

"Hogwash! I work for cash only and everyone in this town knows it and obliges."

She patted his hand. "Of course, dear." She turned to her husband, who stared at her with a raised brow. "Darling, he'll take cash."

"I already knew his terms, Lily. Darling, I need to see you please." His voice was urgent.

She turned to David. "Keep working, David. I'll go see what Ben wants and bring you something cool to drink."

She gave him a hug and scurried off. David knew why. Ben was always whisking his wife off behind closed doors in the middle of the morning, daytime and evening hours. He shook his head and began to hammer harder.

Lily had been a lost cousin of sorts. When word had spread to Fort Worth about Lily being stalked by a rich cattle rustler, his parents admitted she was a relative. David's father and Lily's father were brothers on the outs, so when Lily's parents died, David's father should have taken Lily in. Instead, he pretended she never existed. David never did find out why the two brothers never spoke to each other.

Lily never knew she had an Uncle in Fort Worth. Or, a cousin who looked a lot like her. When David defied his father's wishes to meet his cousin, there was no doubt the two were related. It had been a year now that he had come to town and never left.

Then he met Sylvia.

David sighed.

He had fallen head over heels in love. She was beautiful with her blonde hair and lady-like demeanor. He loved taking her on long buggy rides even though she complained of the heat. Sylvia had dated him for months, proclaiming her love, thinking he had money like his brother-in-law Ben. Then she found out he had no money except what his business earned. She dropped him like a hot potato.

In a matter of weeks she became the wife of banker Randal T. Sharp. When Sylvia and Randal had announced their engagement, it left David to spit in the dirt at their hasty wedding. It happened so fast it had made David's head spin.

He finished fixing the loose floor board, checking the area for more. He spotted another weak spot close to the front door and got to work. It wouldn't do him any good to complain about a lost love. Sylvia had been money hungry and wouldn't have settled for less. It was a dang shame, he liked having someone to care about.

But he knew better than to ever trust a woman again.

An hour later, Lily swept into the room as if she had only been gone for ten minutes. "I'm sorry to have kept you waiting, cousin, here is your drink."

David took a swig of the sweet drink, amused. "Now that I have your attention, tell me what you need done for this Christmas Ball."

He knew she was going to put a lot on him and he didn't mind one bit. Keeping himself busy would help to forget about Sylvia's betrayal.

"David? David, are you day dreaming again? Don't give that harlot one more thought. There is someone out there for you, I promise."

David snapped out of his dark thoughts. Lily always had a way of reading his mind. He shook himself, pushing up from where he had been kneeling on the floor fixing the loose board. "Is it that obvious? I guess you're right, it's time to move on."

"It's only obvious to me, since I know you so well. Look at my life and how it turned around. Yours will, too. Perhaps at the Christmas Ball."

He shrugged. It would do no good to hope. Sylvia had used him and thrown him away like an old goose going to slaughter. There was no point in trying to find anyone else. He vowed to never look at another lady with interest again, in case she'd be another one like Sylvia.

David may have been naive the first time around, but from now on, he was going to be as tough as the hammer he held in his hand.

"David, are you paying attention?" Lily's voice interrupted his thoughts. "I have so many surprises for the first annual Christmas Ball the townsfolk will think royalty has come to town."

David smiled. He needed to keep all the negative thoughts away and help his cousin with her party. "I'm paying attention, Lily. You are right, it's time to move on and forget about Sylvia."

Lily stomped her toe and yelped. "Do not mention that name again. It's a shame we have to invite them to the Ball. Will you be okay to see them together?"

He shrugged. "I doubt I will attend the actual Ball. If I don't see her I should be fine."

"Nonsense! You will attend and perhaps I may find a single lady to attend with you."

"No! Don't you dare, Lily. I appreciate the thought but I'm not ready yet. I told you I will never marry, not any more and I mean what I say."

Lily shrugged. "Whatever you say, David."

David stared. She was up to no good and he knew her well enough to say so. "Lily, I am not kidding. I am not interested in going to the ball with anyone."

"It's fine, David. Do not concern yourself with details. Now, let's see. I have my lists all made out. You will be so amazed at the invitations I'm having made at the newspaper. Daniel Ashwood is printing special ones for me."

"That's wonderful. I have to go to Doc James office to fix a window. How soon will you need me for your next project?"

Lily smiled. "Well, I have the greatest idea on earth!"

David closed his eyes. Lily's ideas were enormous. "Okay, Lily, out with it!"

She swung around in a full circle. "I can't hand out simple invitations to such a wonderful Christmas Ball now, can I?"

"Um, yes. You most certainly can."

"No, David, that would never bode well. I have to make it so extra-ordinary, people will by dying to get here."

David grinned. "They will be dying to get here no matter what type of party you have, Lily. Everyone loves your parties."

She rolled her eyes. "I know David, but, I have a special request to ask of you."

He stilled. "What?"

She reached behind the desk, pulling out a bundle and handed it over.

He stared at the pile of clothing in her arms. "What in the world is this?"

Lily smiled. "This is to be worn by the, uh, Town Crier! Isn't it a grand idea to have our very own representative hand out the invitations? Which I have to pick up today. If you don't mind coming in early tomorrow, then we'll get you all suited up and send you on your way to distribute them."

David shook his head. "You want me to wear this outfit to deliver invitations? There are little bells on the collar of the shirt!"

"Oh, David, I need your help. Please! This is going to be the biggest ball this side of the Mississippi. I do need your cooperation. Who else can I trust to make this all work?"

When Lily wanted her way, she batted her eyes and gave a pouty look that made it hard to refuse. But he wasn't her husband. He was her cousin and had no plans to wear a Town Crier outfit to deliver silly invitations. "There's no way I'm wearing that! I'll deliver your invitations but I will not wear that darned suit!"

<><>

David scowled. How did she talk him into this? He stood in the middle of the foyer of the hotel looking like something out of Victorian England.

Ben and his brother Dawson, who was the Land Title Agent for Wichita Falls, walked in. Ben grimaced. "Lily must be getting ready to send out the invitations. Sorry, David."

David turned, his face unreadable. "Why are you sorry? I am standing here like an idiot, wearing a pair of Harvey plaid knickers and a black bow tie. Do you see what she sewed on to the collar of this shirt? Tiny bells so I jingle when I walk."

Ben and Dawson tried hard not to laugh. When Dawson's lip began twitching, David gathered up the box of invitations and stormed outside before they had a chance to laugh in his face.

David stopped short when he saw the buggy Lily told him to take. The horse had bells hanging from its reins. Garland and little silver and gold balls covered the buggy. They were even attached to the wheels of the buggy so every time the wheels turned the garland flapped in the wind.

Funny she was absent this morning. Leaving a note at the front desk, Lily claimed to be busy working on another project. Her instructions were clear. Take the buggy out front to the surrounding farms and ranches and to Mill Ridge. There was no way he was going to drive to Mill Ridge looking like something out of the Victorian Era.

Three hours later, David had delivered the last of the invitations in Mill Ridge. Even though there was some snivelling and laughing behind his back, mostly by the men of Mill Ridge, the sheriff included, the women and children got a big kick out of him.

He realized he enjoyed making them happy. The smiles and cheers of the little ones clutched at his heart strings.

Doc Hart's wife was directly in front of him, lugging a giant basket across the street. David stopped the buggy to jump out and help. "Mrs. Hart, can I carry that for you?"

When she let him take it he caught some movement under the blanket. "What's in there?"

"A passel of puppies. Millie had a litter a few weeks ago. We were out visiting but it's time to get them back to their mother."

He had no idea who Millie was but nodded anyway. He carried the basket to the front porch. A large black dog peeked through the glass window, barking when she saw what he had in his hands. "This must be Millie."

"Yes, she is wanting her puppies. And you must be Santa's elf," she told him, a large smile on her face.

"I'm the Town Crier. I gave your invitation to your husband."

"I've heard rumors of this ball. We will be happy to attend."

David was glad to be heading back to Wichita Falls. He tipped his wool tweed cap. "Good day, Mrs. Hart."

On the ride back, David threw his hat on the seat beside him. He took off the black bow tie and opened the first button on the too-tight shirt. Glad it was over, he was amazed he went this far to help Lily. She could've hired anyone to do this but chose him, probably to keep him busy and take his mind off things. He laughed out loud. Family helped family even if it made him look silly. At least the kids loved his costume.

He picked up an invitation. The parched paper was rolled up like a scroll. Lily's idea was brilliant. He took off the little ribbon she had tied on the scroll and began to unroll it.

Here Ye! Here Ye!

Your attendance is required at the first annual

Wichita Falls Christmas Ball.

Food, Drinks & Entertainment!
Kris Kringle for the children!
A special guest for your musical entertainment!
Entrance Requirements:
Bring a gift to support the town of Wichita Falls.
Small or large, it can be anything at all, but it must benefit the townsfolk or a family in need.
Your Hosts:
Ben & Lily Sloan
The Location:
The Ballroom at the Wichita Falls Hotel
5:00 Sharp
There will be rooms to stay the night for those from out of town!

David was impressed. Lily had gone all out this time. It was her style and he would do whatever it took to help her. He grinned. Even wearing this silly outfit was worth it to make her happy. He loved his cousin. They had a bond like no other. He'd always watch out for her, unlike his own father who had ignored his duty to take her in when her folks died.

The gushing waterfalls that led to town were a sight for sore eyes. He was going to rid himself of this outfit the moment he dropped the buggy off at the hotel.

As he turned the corner, all kinds of chaos reined in the streets of Wichita Falls. Men were running towards the train depot. A crowd gathered at the steps. The sheriff stood on the platform directing men. A few on horseback began to head down the tracks and out of sight.

David parked the buggy and headed towards the depot, grabbing his small set of tools he always carried along no matter where he went. He pulled the leather pouch from underneath the seat.

"What's happening?" He directed his question to Doc James who caught up to him as they made their way towards the depot.

"Not sure, but I imagine a train car may have derailed."

David noticed the doctor had his black medical bag. His wife, Nurse Ellie, caught up to them.

"Train got robbed, folks! We need all the help we can muster up! I sent the deputy to collect men from the Montgomery ranch." Sheriff Montana pointed to Dawson Sloan. "Dawson, you and Ben head up to Max Ward's ranch and gather up as many wagons as possible. I'm not sure how many people are aboard. Or hurt."

Or dead. Doc James burst through the crowd. "I can help. If someone can loan me a horse, we'll head there now."

One of the townsfolk handed over his horse, offering to help get a wagon with the Sloan brothers.

The sheriff whistled. "Attention folks! The rest of you get saddled up. We need all the muscle we can muster."

David didn't hesitate. He ran to the stable along with the rest of the men. Horses had already been saddled up by the livery team. It wasn't long before every man galloped full force along the tracks towards the train a mile and a half away.

Chapter 2

"Hand it over, Missy. Now!"

"But it's my mother's locket. I promised her I'd never lose it or give it away."

The man leaned down, removing the scarf from his face revealing his scraggly whiskers. Hot, putrid breath rent through the air, almost making her gag.

"I said hand it over before I rip it from your neck!"

Her hands trembled as she slid the necklace over her head. She held it in her grasp longer than the outlaw expected.

"I can't just give it to you. My mother will turn in her grave when she finds out I did such a horrible thing!"

The man growled. He moved even closer, clasping his gloved hands around her own. The locket pinched her skin. "You got spunk but this here is a robbery and I got exactly sixty seconds to finish up what I'm doing. Now give me the locket!"

Coming here was a horrible mistake. She thought it would be better. After the horrible bully her husband turned out to be she was almost relieved he had died six months earlier. What a horrible thought at a time like this but wasn't it just as bad as having a lying, stealing and cheating husband?

He had taken everything they owned and gambled it away. Their money, home, her inheritance, every piece of jewelery and china her mother had left her. It was all gone. Except for this locket.

Now, a rotten, no good, dirty-smelling train robber wanted her locket. The only thing she had left. Well, almost. She had one precious thing that no one was going to take away. It was why she boarded this train in the first place.

"I will not give you my mother's locket. Go steal from someone else." Her nose went up in the air as she stared down the beady-eyed bandit.

His nose twitched and his mouth puckered. Someone called out to hurry up. The outlaw raised his hand. A gun stared her in the face. Stark fear rippled up and down her spine like a rattler about to strike but she would not release it from her fist.

He turned the pistol over and smacked her on the forehead. Holly's eyes widened in surprise. The blunt end of the pistol hitting her skin whipped her head back. Stars flashed before her eyes. She had thought something like this only happened in the pages of the dime novels she loved. No way it was true but here she was, experiencing it first hand. A dark cloud formed as the outlaw jerked her hand. She knew he took her last tie with her mother but was helpless to prevent his thievery.

If it was the last thing she did it would be to hunt that dirty bandit down and get her necklace back. Oh, who was she kidding? No use pretending. The truth was she was a widow fighting for her freedom and she didn't have a soul to help her now. The dark cloud got blacker. Her vision was fading as the dizziness took over. She tried to take deep breaths but it didn't work.

Holly vowed she'd find this awful man and get her precious necklace back. Knowing she was about to faint, she reached for her stomach.

<> <>

David and the others rode hell bent for leather until the train came into view. There were some passengers standing along side the train, while others were still inside. Once the rescuers got closer it was plain to see the large boulder across the tracks. Typical sign of train robbers!

Sheriff Montana motioned for everyone to stop. "Let's make sure they're gone before we barge in." He made his way to the passengers who were standing alongside the train. After speaking with one man, he motioned for everyone to come closer.

David knew it was a matter of time before the next train came barrelling down the track this evening. The men had to move the boulder off the tracks first before anything else was done, otherwise there would be a collision.

More and more wagons began to show up. Cowboys from the Montgomery ranch brought their available wagons. The sheriff ordered the passengers to load up. "Keep them moving," he told the wagon drivers. "Get everyone back to Wichita Falls."

"Take them to the hotel!" Ben ordered the drivers. Some of the passengers were trying to find their carpetbags. The train robbers had gone through many of them, leaving clothes and personal items strewn all over the passenger car.

Workers from Max Ward's ranch brought many more wagons. Max led the men on his dark stallion. "What can we do?" he asked the sheriff.

The two men talked while David helped to roll the boulder from the tracks. It took a large group of men twenty minutes to get it far enough away from the steel tracks it wouldn't be a menace for the next train. He noticed the gunpowder trail leading up the slight hill towards a pile of large boulders. "Looks like they used dynamite to bust this one free." The large boulder had then rolled down the hill in front of the train.

Even Reverend Connors had jumped in to help. "Lucky for the passengers, it may have been a lot worse."

David agreed. The last wagon, the one the reverend had driven, sat by itself as the other wagons and buggys rolled towards Wichita

Falls with frightened, travel weary passengers. "We best get this train moving. I'll go see if they need any help."

David spoke to the engineer, who had been fuming at the fact his train was robbed. "Is there anything I can do?"

The engineer nodded. "My fireman got hurt, he's sitting there with a bullet through his shoulder but he can tell you what to do."

David squatted down where the fireman sat slumped against the wall. "Did you have the doc take a look at this?"

The fireman nodded. "Yup. He said I was darn lucky it just grazed my shoulder. Can't move my arm though. I'll need you to feed the fire for me. Feeling a bit dizzy."

David spent the next half hour following instructions. Before they knew it, he had fed the fire enough so the heat turned the water to steam in order for the engineer to regulate the amount of steam moving through the pistons. The chuff, chuff sound as the powerful train rolled down the tracks gave David great satisfaction. He kept feeding the fire at the other man's direction until they safely pulled into the station at Wichita Falls.

The sheriff had sent most of the passengers to the hotel. David helped the fireman off the train. "The man's hurt. Doc James checked him earlier but I imagine he'll need bandaged up."

Sheriff Montana nodded. "I'll get him to the docs. You mind loading the passenger belongings in the wagon and bring 'em round to the hotel?" The Sheriff turned to the engineer. "Go on down to Jenna's café. She's got some hot soup waiting for you before you move on."

The engineer didn't ask twice. David headed to the passenger car where clothes and belongings were strewn everywhere. Another volunteer pulled a wagon alongside, helping to gather up everyone's belongings to drop off at the hotel.

As a last pass through, David walked down the aisle, making sure they had everyone's stuff. He shook his head at the mess the bandits had left behind. At the very back of the car he heard a soft moan. "What was that?"

Another ranch hand followed behind. "I hear it, too."

"Is there someone on the train?" David asked. He held his hand up, motioning for the other man to be careful.

"There she is."

David found a woman on the floor tucked under the last bench. Soft moans escaped her lips. She was covered in black soot so it was hard to see her. Even though it was hard to see her, how did the others get off the train without noticing she was here? "Help me get her out."

The two men pulled her out as gently as possible. She wore a heavy, ragged coat that covered her gown. It seemed odd to be wearing so much even for a Texas winter, where the nights got cool but not freezing cold.

David hoisted her in his arms. Now that she was out from under the bench he noticed the black soot was dark red and not soot after all. Blood was caked on her face from a wound on her forehead. "Looks like she's been pistol-whipped. Quick, let's get her to the doc."

Without missing a step, David carried the woman from the train, leaving the depot and everyone's belongings behind. He practically ran down the street to the doctor's office. There were several others on the porch, pale and in shock from the train robbery, but no one was wounded, not like this. The doctor worked from the porch, checking each passenger and sending them back to the hotel.

Nurse Ellie moved people out of the way when she saw he was carrying someone. She quickly motioned him inside and made room on the table, assessing their new patient. "Let's get this wound cleaned up. David, can you please tell Doctor James to come in here?"

By the time David came back, Nurse Ellie had a bowl of water by the woman's side, clearing the blood from her face. He stared down at her. Long, thick eyelashes grazed her pale skin. A gash covered her forehead, along the seam of dark, wavy hair. A bump stuck out below, no doubt where the gun had struck her. She was so beautiful even with a wound. Something tightened in his gut, as if he felt her pain.

David backed out the door. "I'll step outside to wait. Let me know when you are done. I'll make sure she gets to the hotel with the rest of the passengers," he told Nurse Ellie, who nodded.

Even though David wasn't responsible for the dark-haired lady, he wanted to wait to make sure she was okay. Pacing back and forth on the porch was drawing the attention of some of the others. "That your wife?"

He shook his head. "No, I found her under a bench in the back of the train car."

"She's a brave one. Stood up to the outlaw!"

David eyed the man. "How so?"

Another one of the passengers interrupted. "It wasn't bravery, it was plain dumb to stand up to that train robber! Went and got herself hurt. There he was, an ugly son-of-a-gun with a gun in his hand and all she cared about was some silly piece of jewelery. She should've gave it to him, instead when she refused he hit her with the backside of his gun and took the darn thing. I was in the seat in front of them, heard it all."

Anger welled up inside David. What kind of a man hits a woman? And with a gun? He stared down the man telling the tale. Why hadn't he helped her afterwards if he was so close by? "What kind of man lets a woman lie there unconscious?"

The man's lip quivered. "Everything happened so fast! We were told to place our head in our laps and not look up for thirty minutes. So, that's what we did."

David swore. He wanted to drive a fist down the man's throat, let him get a taste of how it feels to take a beating to the face. The poor woman got hit, slumped to the floor and in all the commotion was left in between two seats when everyone else got off the train. It appeared as if the cut on her face happened when she struck the floor. Not a soul stopped to help her. He thought at first she was hidden from view but now he knew better. The ones who saw her left her there.

David continued to stare at the man. "I hope you plan to get back on that train."

He nodded. "Sure do. Just as soon as I see the doctor."

"Good riddance," he mumbled. They didn't need cowards like him in Wichita Falls. Turning his back, David leaned against the porch, waiting for the doctor.

Granted, the woman had been foolish during a train robbery but there was no excuse for the man sitting on the bench to leave the train without checking to see if she was hurt. He had ignored her, forgotten her like she was already dead.

He turned back to glare at the man, who now hung his head. Served him right, David thought. He hoped the man's guilt kept him up all night.

Doc James came back out to tend to the ones who were left. He caught David's attention. "She'll be ready to move shortly. Do you have someone to help get her to the hotel?"

He shook his head, glaring back at the man who refused to help her on the train. "Nope. Ain't no one here worthy enough to help. I'll do it myself."

The doctor seemed confused at his words but didn't ask questions. "Very good. Make sure to follow Nurse Ellie's instructions. Looks like she won't be able to travel for some time."

David wondered why. He went back inside to escort her to the hotel. Knocking on the open door to the office, he peeked inside. She was still lying on the table, minus her heavy coat. His eyes widened when he realized why.

The woman was with child. His gaze went to her left hand, searching for a wedding band. Disappointment surged through him when a gold band stood out like a sore thumb. He had been so intent on getting her here he hadn't noticed she was married. "Where is her husband?"

Nurse Ellie shot him a look. "Dead. She came to some time ago so I asked her where he is considering the circumstances. She mumbled something about how the lying, stealing man was dead and she wasn't sorry one bit. He had ruined her life."

Why did David feel relief at this strangers remark. Why was she traveling alone this time of year? Where did she come from? "What else did she say?"

Nurse Ellie began to clean up. "That was it," she grinned. "James wants her to rest and not have any added stress. She took a severe thump on the head. Such trauma may cause the baby to come at any time. Wherever she was going, she'll have to wait until the baby arrives."

"I'll move her to the hotel. I'm sure my cousin Lily will make room for her."

Why did David feel obliged to make sure this woman was taken care of? It didn't make any sense.

A soft hand touched his shoulder. "It's all right to feel something, David. You have a kind soul. Don't let what happened keep you from caring about someone else. Sylvia was not worthy of you."

He turned to stare at Nurse Ellie. Did he wear his heart on his sleeve that everyone thought he was still hankering for the banker's wife? He was angry, not hurt. Fearful of loving again, not in love with that harlot. If anything, he despised her more than he ever loved her. "I am not afraid to care about someone else."

"Is that why you hide in your work day and night?" She spoke softly, her voice soothing. She was a good nurse with the heart and voice of an angel. Her calm demeanor was reassuring but he didn't like to discuss his feelings with anyone.

He shrugged. "I suppose. Right now, I'm going to take this young lady to my cousin's hotel. I am doing this solely out of duty for my fellow man."

Nurse Ellie smiled. "Of course. I'll be right along. After you get her settled, we'll go over her ritual for the next few days. She will need watched over carefully."

When David picked her up to carry her to the hotel, she let out a small whoosh of air. Her eyelids fluttered and then she stared straight at him before snuggling against his chest as if she belonged there. She didn't open her eyes the whole time he walked up the street.

Lily came running when David carried her inside the hotel. "Oh my! Let's get her to a room upstairs. David, take her to the second floor suite."

As he made his way upstairs, Lily belted out orders to the others like a sailor getting ready to set out on a long trip. He found the honeymoon suite empty so deposited her on the oversize bed. Picking up a small blanket from the bottom, David covered her up.

He stared down at her. He didn't even know her name.

Her eyes fluttered open. Long, black lashes bounced off her pink cheeks. Dark eyes stared back at him.

"Hello," he said, not knowing what else to say.

She snuggled deeper in the cover, smiling. "Hello. You must be one of Santa's elves. Thank you for rescuing me."

David took a step back. "What! An elf?" He looked like an elf? That was the most ridiculous thing he ever heard until he looked down to see tiny bells hanging on the collar of his once white shirt. He had forgotten about the Town Crier outfit his cousin had made him wear.

"Yes, my very own elf. How lovely. Thank you for rescuing me."

David didn't know what to say. He grinned. "If you say I'm an elf, then so be it. Get some rest. The nurse will be along shortly."

She wasn't paying attention. Her hands went to her neck. Her lips began to quiver, then she stared him in the eye. "Where is my locket? Did that no good, stinking, robbing outlaw take my locket after all?"

"I heard you put up a good fight, that's why you are here instead of loading up on the train right now with the others."

"What! I'm going to miss my stop? No, I have to be on the train!" She struggled to sit up.

David stepped forward, placing a hand on her arm. "Doc James said you were not to get excited, else the baby may come early. Rest is what he ordered."

She closed her eyes. "Of course. I know, the baby," she whispered, her angelic voice so soft he leaned forward to hear her words. "I won't let anything happen to the baby."

She looked up at him then, gratitude pouring from her beautiful eyes. "You saved me. Thank you."

Nurse Ellie chose that exact moment to enter. She carried a small basket. Placing it on the bedside table, she turned to the woman. "I see you are awake. That's good, you will need to stay that way for the rest of the day. We want to make sure there was no other damage."

David grimaced. Her forehead was turning dark purple. It seemed to have gotten worse since the doc stitched her wound.

Nurse Ellie patted his shoulder. "Thank you for all your help, David."

The woman turned to stare. "Your name is David? Thank you again for saving me."

He grinned.

When she smiled, David took a step back. He had thought Sylvia was a beautiful woman until he learned just how ugly she was inside. This woman, was she like Sylvia? He didn't want to return the smile then found his mouth turning up against his will. "It was nothing. When anyone needs help, we help."

She reached out a fragile hand, the one with the wedding ring on her finger. Spellbound, he moved towards her, taking her hand in his own. He stared at the gold ring.

She must have noticed. "He's gone. Dead. I wore the rings so I wasn't a target riding the train alone."

"It's not a good thing to ride unchaperoned."

She smiled. He was captivated when her lips parted. A dimple creased in her left cheek. He wanted to kiss her.

"I've read many dime novels so I knew what to expect from the varmints and rowdy cowboys. It's why I wore my dead husband's wedding rings. Which, by the way, were won in a game of chance. Can you believe he gambled for these rings? It's about the only thing he actually won."

She tried to take off the ring. As if in slow motion, David helped her. It slid from her dainty finger without a problem. "A game of chance?" he questioned.

She nodded. "My dead husband was a gambler. A cheat. A rotten, stinking no-good -"

"I think we get the drift," Nurse Ellie spoke up.

David placed the ring on the bedside table.

"You can throw that thing out the window."

"You may need it when you get back on the train." When she was able to is what he meant.

Nurse Ellie was adamant about her staying put until she delivered the baby and told her so. "Right now, you are staying put, young lady. There is a small baby to think about and your own health."

Lily, full of grace and energy, swept into the room. "Hello, I'm Lily. I own this hotel with my husband, Ben. Now, I don't want you to worry about a thing. We'll have Nurse Ellie check on you daily and you have this room until you are better and the baby comes along."

She tried to sit up but failed. "I don't know what to say. No one has ever been this kind to me before."

Lily laughed, her poetic voice lightening the mood. "That's because you've never been to Wichita Falls before. Who knows, you may not want to leave." With those words, Lily turned on her heels and left, winking to her cousin.

David wondered what she was up to. Lily had watched with raised eyebrows when he brought the woman inside. He had been concerned, yes, but it was as a good neighbor should. There was nothing more to this than helping one another. He hoped Lily wasn't trying to make more out of his kindness.

Nurse Ellie instructed him to sit by her side for awhile, to make sure she stayed awake. "I don't believe it will hurt any if she falls asleep but we like to be careful. She took a hard blow to the head. It'd be best to keep her awake for the rest of the day."

"I may be needed elsewhere." Although, he liked the idea of sitting with her.

"I imagine so. I'll go talk to Lily, see if she can send someone up to replace you. As long as the door stays wide open, I don't believe there will be any talk. After all, she is wounded. I need to get back to the doctor's office."

"He's an elf," the woman mentioned.

Nurse Ellie burst out laughing. She picked up her case. "With those bells on his collar, he certainly does look like one."

David glared at Nurse Ellie. She wasn't helping any. "I'm not an elf. I'm a Town Crier."

He watched as Nurse Ellie and the woman glanced at each other then tried to keep from laughing.

David positioned a chair at the bedside. He didn't know what to say now that they were alone.

She sighed. "This is nice. It's the first soft bed I've been in since leaving home."

He looked at her. Long, thick hair blanketed the pillow. He wanted to run his fingers through the dark waves. "Where is home?"

"A bustling city you may have heard of. New York."

He raised an eyebrow. "What are you doing here? Alone, if I may ask."

She shrugged. "Making my way westward to a new life for me and the baby and -"

She had clamped her mouth shut before finishing her sentence. She was beautiful. Yet, another woman he didn't trust. There was no sense in letting his heart fall for this one even though he seemed drawn to her. She had stopped talking all of a sudden. What was she holding back? He wanted to give her the benefit of the doubt, after all, it was the holiday season. "And?"

She shook her head. Smiling, she batted her dark lashes and looked up at him. "And, nothing else. I am tired." She feigned a yawn.

"Nurse Ellie said you weren't to fall asleep. Perhaps you may want to prop up the pillows and sit up for a bit."

She nodded. "That will be nice. Do you mind?" The innocent look she gave melted him. Darn it, this wasn't working. He had to remain heartless when it came to her. Otherwise, he'd fall in the same trap he had with Sylvia.

Maybe her name was Sylvia, too. He had to ask. "You've never told us your name."

She leaned forward as he pumped the pillows, moving them so her back was leaning against them. "It's Holly. Holly Bell."

"Welcome to Wichita Falls, Holly Bell."

Relief flooded through him when Daniel Ashwood's wife, Charity, knocked on the door. Now, maybe he could escape. "Are you here to sit with Miss Bell?"

Charity held a small pad in her hand. "Yes, and you are wanted in the lobby. Lily has some men bringing in wood for the stage. You go on, I'll take over here." Charity turned away to introduce herself.

David escaped as quickly as he could. He took one look back as if regretting his decision but he didn't have the inclination to fall for another beautiful woman. Not now. Not ever.

Chapter 3

Holly watched the man leave. He had the funniest outfit on she had ever seen. Almost like he was in the theatre.

"What's so funny?" the newswoman asked. Charity had introduced herself as the most famous newswoman in Texas. She scooted the chair even closer to the bed than David had.

Holly smiled. "When I came to after that darn, no-good robbing thief cold-cocked me with his gun, I saw David standing there, watching me. He pulled me from the train and carried me to the doctor's office. Everything was fuzzy then but when I finally focused, there he was, dressed like an elf, although he claims to be a Town Crier."

They both burst into giggles.

Charity grinned. "I believe he thinks he is a Town Crier but I'm pretty certain Lily wanted him to look like an elf. I doubt David noticed the difference. He seems quite embarrassed to be wearing the outfit."

After that, it was so easy to talk with Charity. She kept Holly's mind off her troubles. Hearing stories of how Charity became the top reporter in the area to some of the townsfolk's troubles made hers seem small in the whole scope of things. After some time, she realized Wichita Falls was a town she would love to be a part of. If only she hadn't accepted the mail order proposal from Guy Worthrop. He was expecting her in California, where she would become a gold miner's wife. She had promised to keep his house while he was away working the mines. Holly thought it was a great deal.

"What are you thinking?" Charity asked, disturbing her thoughts.

"You are very observant, but, you don't want to know."

"Actually, I do want to know. It's my life's work to get people to open up." She stuck her pencil behind her ear. "But since I consider you a friend now we are off the record. Why the frown?"

"I can't talk about it right now. I'm tired. I better get some rest."

"No rest for the weary," Lily announced, holding a tray as she bustled her way in. "Charity, that will enough questioning our guest for the day. Besides, love, I want to have a glass of wine with you before you leave. We've lots to talk about."

"Ah, you've got some dirt on someone? Very good." Charity turned to Holly. "Lily has the scoop of what's going on in this town. If it's happening here at the hotel, she knows all about things. I love having a glass of wine with her each week."

Lily settled the tray on Holly's lap. "I've asked David to check on you before he leaves. He's building a stage for a special guest who will be arriving Christmas eve. I will tell you, Holly, this place is going to be quite busy for some time. We're having a great Christmas Ball in two weeks and the preparations are beginning already."

Holly sighed. "Sounds lovely. I'm afraid I'll be on my way to San Francisco. I've been promised to a gentleman."

"You are a mail order bride!" Both ladies spoke at once. "So were we!"

Holly burst into tears. She placed both hands over her face to try to hold in the sobs. Charity and Lily hurried to her side, patting her back and shoulders until she settled down. A white hanky appeared out of nowhere.

Holly grabbed it and dabbed her eyes. "I'm so sorry."

Charity shook her head. "No need to be. We were in your spot, you know. It isn't easy being a mail order bride."

The two women were easy to talk to. Just then, another woman tip-toed inside. Charity and Lily both shouted at once. "Ruby!"

The three ladies hugged as Holly looked on. Was Ruby another mail-order bride? Perhaps they may give her tips. If it were up to her, she'd never want to marry again but didn't have much of a choice.

Lily introduced Ruby. "This is the first mail order bride in our group to come to Wichita Falls. Actually, Miss Addie is but that's a whole other generation and story. We will fill you in at some point. Holly, welcome to Wichita Falls. You may not want to leave here."

Sadly, fate had other things in store. If Holly didn't marry Guy Worthrop, her four sisters would never get out of the children's home her nasty husband had forced them into. She sat back, no longer hungry. Mr. Worthrop had promised to take her in knowing she was a widow with child. He had also promised to pay to have her sisters sent to San Francisco after she arrived safely.

According to the children's home, in order to get her sisters, she had to have a husband and a reliable home first. So, the two had struck a deal. Mr. Worthrop provides a home and marriage and she keeps house while he is gone mining. It seemed perfect, almost too good to be true.

Holly had a hard time trusting a stranger but he had sounded kind in his many letters. Her eyes began to skirt the room, looking for her carpetbag.

"What's wrong, Holly? You look upset. I think Nurse Ellie said not to let anything upset you."

"My things? I had a carpetbag with my initials clearly marked on top. I don't see it here."

Lily gave her a hug. "Don't fret. I'll have David take a look. There's still some things downstairs. I'm sure your bag is there."

Relief flooded through her. If she didn't have her ticket, she'd be stuck here with no means to get to San Francisco. She used up every single dime she had except for a few dollars stuffed in her boot. The matchmaker in New York City had warned her to always hide money on her person. At least it was a relief to have a few dollars of her own.

"We better go. Ladies, come along." Lily gave Holly a hug, followed by Charity and Ruby. They left her to stare at a bowl of broth.

She waited anxiously for over an hour until David knocked on the door. "Please come in," she told him.

He held her carpetbag in his hand. It looked so small against his big, muscular arm. "I believe this belongs to you." He pointed to her initials on the front.

"Thank you!" Holding her arms out, she grazed his hand while accepting the bag. Warm fingers brushed against her own. A spark ignited inside of her, an unusual feeling since her own husband hadn't ever made her feel anything like this. Even though a child was conceived it was not from love but from duty. Now, she felt nothing for him except anger and bitterness. He had lost it all and left her to pick up the pieces.

David watched her with steady eyes, which seemed to calm her somewhat. She looked away quickly, digging into her carpet bag. Everything was askew, clothes thrown haphazardly in the bag. A few items weren't even hers. She sat back and sighed, unable to find what she needed the most.

"Is there a problem?"

She nodded. "I'm afraid so. My train ticket is gone. I'm afraid without that, I can't board the train."

"You can always get another ticket."

She shook her head. "I don't have enough money. The ticket was purchased with the last of my cash except for a few dollars. I'm afraid I'm stuck here."

David frowned. "Is there anyone you can wire a request to? We do have the telegraph office now, you know."

Perhaps Guy Worthrop would wire her money for the train ride there. Although when they exchanged letters, he had mentioned all of his money was tied up in a gold mine. He asked her to buy a ticket and he'd reimburse her when she got there. She thought that was an unusual request. He had been under the impression she had her own money, although she never claimed to. Maybe it was her home address. It was considered a well-to-do area by most standards.

Six months had been a long time to watch everything wilt away and be taken away as if it never meant anything. First, they came for her furniture. Then, her home. When her bank accounts were frozen, she turned to her mother-in-law, who refused to help stop the foreclosures.

Holly had inherited her parents home when they died in a street car accident. Her father had been a prominent attorney in the city and had a nice brownstone on Fifth Avenue. Holly and her four younger sisters were devastated when her parents were killed but she vowed to take care of them. Charles had worked in the law firm where her father was a partner.

Charles Bell had quickly swept her off her feet, promising to take care of her and her sisters when her parents had died. Instead of purchasing another home, they decided to keep her parents home, which made more sense. Except the moment he moved into her family home, the gambling began.

There were some sweet times when he treated her like a princess. But it didn't last longer than a few months. By the time she found out he was a gambler, it was too late. His death had revealed it all. By that time she was already three months pregnant. He had been a charmer, hiding everything, pretending to work late at night while in the gambling houses losing everything they had.

Holly vowed to never trust another man again. But when they foreclosed on her home she was forced to send her sisters to a children's home, promising them she would get them back. Since Sister Mary Ellen was a friend of her mothers, she told Holly she'd keep them from the Mercy Train until the end of the year. After that, they'd be separated and sent to various homes. Holly feared if she didn't get them in time, she'd never see her sisters again.

She came up with a plan when she saw the newspaper ad from a local match-making agency. The only course she had was to become a mail order bride. It had to be a man of honor who would accept all five of them and the unborn baby. After several refusals, she accepted Guy Worthrop's proposal. All it cost her was a ticket there and his promise to send for her sisters.

The girls were expecting her to send for them by the end of the year. She had to get to California and soon. She didn't dare let them down, they had gone through enough. Except this little one wasn't due until Christmas eve. Would that give her enough time to recover and get to her destination to marry by the end of the year? It took four days, maybe five at the most to travel the rails from New York to California. Holly was worried she was running out of time.

Holly shook herself when she heard David speaking. "Holly? Did you hear me? I asked if there was anyone you wanted me to contact?"

She nodded. "Yes, there is someone. I'm on my way to San Francisco to be married. I'll need to wire my fiancé, Guy Worthrop. I have a few dollars in my boot to pay for the telegram." She'd have to use the last of her money to send the wire. Leaning over, she pulled off her boot. Her head pounded but she took the small wad of money and placed it in his hand.

"Married? I thought your husband was dead? Remember, that low down, rotten, cheating, lying, well, you get the drift."

He made her smile even in the midst of all the sadness. "He was the cause of my troubles. Yes, he's dead. Run over by his own horse and cart. Drunken louse! I'm forced to marry a man I don't know. It is the only way to get my sisters out of the children's home. I had no choice but to leave them there and follow my plan." It was the only way to give the child inside of her a decent home. The responsibility was overwhelming. Holly's head began to pound more and more. She closed her eyes.

A strong, warm hand cupped her cheek. He slowly turned her face towards him, forcing her to open her eyes. The soft yearning in his own eyes tore at Holly's heartstrings. This man seemed to care and he hardly knew her. Why? Why would a stranger matter so much to her?

"I'm sorry you are going through so much right now. The doctor is right, it's too dangerous for you to take a train. I'll send a telegram on your behalf. What would you like me to say?"

She shivered. Leaning into his warm hand, she wanted to stay there forever. Yet, she knew better. She had responsibilities. "If you have paper, I'll write it down."

David searched for a piece of paper. In the desk drawer he found stationary. After scribbling, erasing and writing more words, she finally set the pencil down. Folding the paper in half, Holly handed it to him.

"I'll be back. You should try to rest."

He was almost out the door when she called to him. He turned. "David, will you truly come back?"

He nodded, a sadness in his eyes she knew well. A desire in his eyes for something he was unable to have.

Holly wanted what her parents had. Her father had been a prominent attorney who didn't spoil his children. He had made them all work hard and appreciate every single thing they had, unlike some others in the same class. They each had chores to do daily even though she was taught to always be the oldest sister and to take care of her siblings. Holly didn't mind. What her parents taught her had paid off. Even though her parents had the unfortunate accident, she was determined to raise the family together.

Family. Honor. Love. It was all she asked for. Her dead husband had taken those things and threw them away with a roll of the dice. His gambling had cost her a home that had been in the family for ages. Little had she known he took out a large mortgage on the brownstone until the banker stood at her door a few months after he had died.

She had been devastated to lose the family home, yet was just as determined to keep them together at all costs. Promising her sisters a short separation, even if she had to give up her happiness or a chance at love, she was determined they would be together. It was just a matter of time.

Holly waited patiently for David to come back with good news.

<> <>

David opened the door where the new telegraph office was housed. He handed the letter over. It was good no one else was in the building since the telegraph operator read back to David what he had typed with the stick punch on to a piece of perforated tape.

Dear Mr. Worthrop. Train robbed. My ticket is gone. Out of money. Send money for a ticket right away or come to Wichita Falls Texas to marry. Time is running out for my sisters. Sincerely. Your mail order bride. Holly Bell.

"Will this be satisfactory, sir?"

"Sounds about right. How long until we can get a response?"

"It depends. This telegram will reach San Francisco in approximately four minutes. It's up to the telegraph operator to locate Mr. Worthrop."

"I believe she wrote the address on the note."

"Yes, I added it to the telegram. Send?"

"Yes. When you get a response, please send for me. Miss Bell is out of commission at the moment. She is laid up at the hotel."

"Is she the young lady that stood up to the train robber?"

"The one. I guess the whole town has heard by now."

The telegraph operator nodded. "Not sure if that was brave or not." He began to count each word.

David placed some bills on the counter. He tucked the small stack she had handed him back in his pocket, knowing it was the last of her money. At least she didn't have to pay for the telegram, he'd taken care of that. After all, this was the holiday season to be kind.

He stepped out of the way when Miss Addie brushed past him. Tipping his hat, David said hello.

"Hello, Mr. Morgan. I hear you've rescued a brave young lady from the train. Tell me, is the gossip I've heard about her correct?"

He didn't know why she asked, she already knew it was. There wasn't much that got past her. People claimed she had eyes in the back of her head. He turned back just to make sure, then grinned when she stared, waiting for an answer.

"Yes, I believe it is. She's resting now at the hotel. Lily has promised to care for her until the baby arrives."

A smile played across Miss Addie's face. "A holiday baby. How perfect. Good day, Mr. Morgan."

David hurried back to the hotel. He wanted to finish the stage for Lily, knowing there was much more to do in order to get ready for the fancy Christmas Ball. Everyone in town was talking about it. Jim Wheeler at the mercantile mentioned his sales had gone up in the last few days with all the ladies buying plenty of material for their ball gowns. He hired David to build him a few more shelves.

He was worried about Holly. He had a strong sense of intuition and knew she didn't want to get married to the man in California. He had heard it in her voice and yet she felt inclined to go through with a loveless marriage for her sister's sake. Maybe the townsfolk of Wichita Falls would help. But, what could they do?

Chapter 4

"Holly, why don't you come downstairs to the festivities? No sense in lying in bed day and night."

Holly knew Lily was right. She had been pouting for the last three days, ever since David stopped by to tell her there was still no word from California. Her headaches were better, even Nurse Ellie told her to get up and move about. "Maybe it will do me some good to get out of this room."

Lily helped her get dressed. She had one other gown to wear, a soft gray that was loosened at the waist. Her belly seemed to have grown in the last three days. Holly laid a hand over her stomach. "I hope she or he soon comes out. I'm getting anxious." Truthfully, even though she was nervous about giving birth, she wanted this baby to hurry so she'd be able to go to San Francisco herself and face her fiancé. Why hadn't he returned the telegram yet?

Lily finished fixing Holly's hair. "There. You look beautiful. I'll set up a chair downstairs by the decorating of the tree so you can watch. How about a cup of hot chocolate to keep you nice and warm? I have the cocoa sent from a special shop in Fort Worth and it's delicious."

"That sounds wonderful." Since she hadn't been out of bed much since the accident, her legs were weak. Holly leaned on Lily as they made their way down the stairs.

The tree had been set upright in the center of the ballroom. David looked up and smiled as she descended down the stairs, immediately by her side to take her elbow. "I've got her, Lily."

Holly didn't miss the way Lily made a face at her cousin. She stuck out her tongue then smiled at Holly. "I'll go get the hot chocolate then."

David settled her in a wing chair beside the empty tree. Someone handed him a small blanket to place over her legs. Children from the town were kneeling and sitting on the floor, picking their favorite decorations to place on the enormous tree. Holly looked around to see others stringing popcorn, the smell permeating across the room. Pine cones and leaves decorated the large windows, while two ladies took red ribbon to make perfect bows to hang around the greenery.

A ladder was pushed against the wall close to the tree. David smiled at her before climbing up to place decorations near the top. A few times she giggled when he pretended to almost fall. The children sucked in their breath and then giggled and clapped as he made them laugh.

"Isn't this lovely?" a tiny voice came out of nowhere.

Holly stretched her neck to see a small couple staring at her. She did a double take, blinking her eyes to make sure they were real. The man and woman were no taller than one of the six year olds in the ballroom. "Yes, this is lovely. Hello."

The man held out his hand. He wore a tailored suit and small bright red bow-tie. The lady wore a colorful festive gown with a hem that trailed behind. No one would ever miss them walking into a room. They were quite strange. "Welcome to Wichita Falls. We're staying at the hotel for the holidays."

She reluctantly shook his hand, wanting to be nice and yet they had her somewhat concerned. The lady pushed her way to stand in front of the man. "Hello, I'm Mrs. Martin. We've heard quite the story about you, Miss Bell."

Holly was having a nice time. She didn't want to think of the train robbery or her bad luck. "I'm sure most of what you heard is true." She shook the woman's hand. "Hello, Mrs. Martin."

They stood beside her, watching the children's antics, laughing as they sipped cognac. Holly hadn't wanted to be rude before but realized she was really enjoying their company after all. It seemed everyone in this town wanted to be nice. David ventured over, finished with his tree escapades. "I see you've met Mr. and Mrs. Martin."

"Yes, they have been keeping me entertained."

"Are you up for a walk? The decorations outside are a site to see, if I say so myself."

Mr. and Mrs. Martin and Holly all laughed. "I would love to see them. I imagine you've had your hand in putting them up?"

"Of course." The two took a walk outside the hotel. Festive greenery was placed on the windows, while the gas street lights were covered with more greens and bows, with pine cones adding to the holiday décor. A large nativity scene was set close to a wooden bench along the front of the hotel.

"Would you like to sit here for awhile?" David asked Holly. He turned to the Martins, inviting them as well.

"We'll be going back in, but you two kids have fun," Mr. Martin told them. "We came along to see the scenery and now we are hungry for some cookies. It was a pleasure to meet you, Miss Bell."

Holly let David lead her to the bench, where they sat watching the other townsfolk come and go. There were couples walking hand in hand through the doors, a few laughing but others with such a serious look Holly mentioned their faces may stay like so. David began to make faces when someone walked by looking prudish.

"You are silly, David," she told him, giggling like a school girl. Holly hadn't laughed like this for such a long time. Not since her sisters and her were all together. Before she realized it, a deep moan escaped.

David immediately took her hand. "What is it, Holly? The baby?"

A tear escaped, rolling down her face before she was able to stop it. "No, it's not the baby. It's, well, it's," she sniffed, feeling rather stupid for ruining such a wonderful night. One moment she's happy and laughing her heart out, the next ridden with sadness.

David took her chin in his hand, swiping at a tear with his other. "Did I say something to make you cry?"

She shook her head. "No, David, you are wonderful. I haven't laughed so much since my sisters and I spent time together during the holidays. The memories came flooding back and it made me so upset. I'm not sure why I haven't received a telegram back from Mr. Wolthrop. He was my one chance to have my sisters with me. Now, I'm not sure what to do. I'm afraid I may have failed them."

Her hands covered her face. David gathered her in his big arms, folding her into his chest. "Shh, everything will turn out fine."

She sobbed into his chest. His warmth comforted her so she stayed there in his arms until the last tear fell. "I'm sorry, David. You've been a good friend. I'm glad we met."

David kept his arms around her. "Friends. That sounds nice."

She looked up at him with regret. If only she wasn't waiting for Mr. Worthrop to whisk her off to California she'd want to get to know David better. He was such a gentleman.

They stared at one another longer than intended. David lowered his head. He was so close she waited for the kiss. She even lifted her face towards him even though she knew it wasn't right since she was someone's mail order bride.

At the last moment she turned away. "I'm sorry, David. I am spoken for."

David lifted a hand to her cheek. His warm hand caused her to close her eyes, leaning into the warmth. If only she weren't going to California. If only he was the man waiting for her at the end of the line. Except the reality was someone else, Guy Worthrop, who was offering to be her husband and help take care of her sisters.

Holly stood. Her sisters were her responsibility. She had to find a way to contact Mr. Worthrop. "Thank you for being my friend, David."

David stood. He nodded. "I understand. I'm sorry to be so forward. Forgive me, Holly."

She took his hands in hers. "I do forgive you. I wish -"

"David! How nice to see you again!" A beautiful blonde-haired woman came towards them on the arm of a well dressed man. His overcoat was long and dark, a large hat covering his hair. When Holly looked closer, she watched the man lift his hat in greeting. He was as bald as one of the chickens after their feathers were plucked.

Trying not to grin, she waited as everyone went through the introductions. David turned to her. "This is Randal T. Sharp and his newly acquired wife, Sylvia Sharp."

Sylvia's smile was so fabricated Holly had wondered what he saw in her except for her beauty. She shook hands only to be nice. Holly heard about his relationship with Sylvia from Lily and Charity yesterday morning. They felt she should know in case someone mentioned it. Why they felt it was important was beyond her. After all, she was friends with David, that was all.

David looked uncomfortable. Holly wanted to save him from the scrutiny. She gave him one of her best smiles. "David, shall we continue on our walk?"

He nodded, tipping his own hat at the two. "Goodnight," he told them, taking her arm as they made their way down the street.

Holly didn't know where they were going and didn't care. It was nice taking a stroll with him by her side. Except, David kept walking as if in a trance. After some time, her legs began to ache. She slowed down when she almost stumbled.

David turned to her. "I'm sorry, Holly, is this too much?"

"I'm afraid my legs are starting to give out on me."

"It's my fault. I had my mind on those two." David surprised her when he lifted her into his arms and carried her back to the hotel. Walking through the door, she clung onto his neck, her face in his chest. She was a bit embarrassed to have every single eyeball in the hotel staring.

Lily ran over. "Is she hurt?"

"No, tired. We took a walk longer than necessary." Holly heard the pain in his voice. He was upset at seeing Sylvia.

Was he still in love with a married woman?

David was upset at himself. If he hadn't been thinking about the troubled conversation earlier today, he would have noticed how far they walked. He took the steps two at a time with Holly in his arms. She needed to rest. It wouldn't do her any good to fall ill again.

After placing her on the bed, David pulled a thin blanket over her. "You get some rest. This was probably too much for your first venture out."

"I'm fine, really. You don't have to fuss so much," Holly told him. Her face was pale even though she said she was fine.

He took her hand. "Thank you for spending time with me. I had a wonderful evening."

Holly tilted her head. She reached up, running her fingers across his cheek.

"So did I, thank you."

David wanted to closed his eyes and imagine she was his wife. He wanted to pretend it was his child. Yet, he knew better. He quickly backed away. "Good night, Holly."

Outside, he stood at the top of the steps, shaken. David had vowed he'd never fall in love, not after Sylvia. His solemn promise to himself that he would spend the rest of his life alone was slowly diminishing. Holly had some magical power that drew him to her. He was falling in love with his new friend. Fast. How did it happen so quickly, like within the blink of an eye?

"David? What are you doing just standing there? Is everything all right?" Mr. and Mrs. Martin stood at the bottom of the stairs looking up at him.

He shrugged, making his way down the steps one at a time. No sense to be in a hurry. The night would not be as fun without Holly to spend time with. He looked beyond the Martins to see Sylvia and her husband making their rounds. Dread filled his soul. He wasn't going to stick around to watch. Even though he no longer had any feelings of love for her, he still resented what she did to him. He would avoid the couple at all costs.

"Let's talk," Mr. Martin told him, taking a firm grip on his arm. Even though David was ready to go home, he didn't protest when the Martins led him to a small alcove at the bottom of the stairs. The others were in the wide open ballroom having a great time decorating. He spotted adults and children alike enjoying the festivities.

Lily had placed a few scattered lounge chairs and a small settee in a private alcove below the open stairs. The three took a seat. His thoughts kept going back to Holly and the news he had learned today.

Mr. Martin steepled his fingers together, staring at him. "Spill it, David. Something has been eating at you all night long. The only time you looked normal was when spending time with the lovely Miss Bell."

"Yes, I am in agreement. Spill the beans, cousin." Lily had wandered over to join the trio.

Charity made her way next. She sat on one of the empty chairs. Then Ruby showed up. Before he knew what was happening, Rebecca, the sheriff's wife and Grace Holloway, the title agent's wife wandered over. When Hannah, Max Ward's wife came in the front door, she spotted the small crowd gathered there and made her way over to her friends. After hugging each person, the other girls explained they were waiting for David to explain why he was so upset.

"Sophie and Ellie just walked in. May as well wait until they arrive. That way we don't have to repeat ourselves more than necessary."

David stared at his cousin.

She shrugged. "We've all been through hard times together. The eight of us are like a family. Mr. and Mrs. Martin here have seen us through some rough times, too. Many times they've been detrimental in making things happen in this town we call home. So, now you are part of our extended family, cousin. If something happens, we all work together to fix it and by the look on your face, you need us!"

The others nodded and reassured David it was so.

Soon, every single person was looking at him. "What? There's nothing wrong!"

"Son, you can pretend to yourself if you want to, but we all know you. You've been hanging your head ever since you got back from the telegraph office. What happened there?"

Was this for real? Was the whole town of Wichita Falls going to gang up on him? No, that wasn't true, the heart of the town wasn't here. He knew all too well, had heard the rumors of how Miss Addie was always interfering in other people's business. Even though it always turned out for the best, he was probably lucky she wasn't present.

"Wait, Miss Addie just arrived." They waved to the older woman, who nodded and swept across the floor like she was entering the King's private chambers.

David held his breath when the front door opened again. If one more person joined them, he'd up and leave no matter how bad he hurt his cousin's feelings. He was starting to feel like he was on display.

Lily spoke up. "Ladies, we have a dilemma. Let's listen while David tells us what is going on."

David ran a hand through his hair. "Lily, this is insane! I'm fine and I wish you'd stop this nonsense."

Everyone stared. David's eyes wandered to the ballroom where children were chasing little puppies. A passel of black, gray and white puppies were jumping and running, making the children squeal with delight.

"Out with it, young man." Miss Addie's voice was gentle but firm. He was drawn to the sound, as if there was no way to stop this from happening.

He was being ambushed. Yet, he needed advice. The situation at hand was beyond anything he had ever dealt with. A long sigh escaped before he realized.

"That's it, son. Out with it, we can't help unless you tell us." Mr. Martin patted his hand.

"I went to check to see if Holly, uh, Miss Bell's telegram came back today."

Lily interrupted. "Ladies, Holly Bell is the guest who confronted the train robber. She is a reluctant mail order bride for those who don't know, heading to California as soon as her baby is born. The only reason she is going through with a loveless marriage is because the groom has promised to take in her four sisters, who are waiting at a children's home in New York City. I found out from Holly she has until the end of the year to get them or they will be sent on the Mercy Train and most likely be separated forever."

Mr. Martin's brow shot up. "What is the name of the home? I may be able to help."

Lily shrugged. "We don't know, you'll have to ask Miss Bell."

Mr. Martin took out a small piece of paper and pencil to scribble on. He tucked it back in his pocket. "No need, I have ways to find out."

David continued, "I'm afraid I am about to crush all her hopes and dreams. She got a telegram today." He reached in his pocket. Unfolding the yellow paper, he handed it to Mr. Martin first. Silence ensued as the telegram was passed around the small group.

Several pairs of eyes widened in shock at the news. Anger seethed from Rebecca, the sheriff's wife. "This is preposterous. How can he let a woman with child high and dry?"

When the telegram finally fell into Miss Addie's hands, she looked read it then peered into David's eyes. "There is only one solution."

David frowned. "I don't have the heart to tell her."

Miss Addie's brow shot up. "Who says you have to tell her? All she is wanting for Christmas is someone to marry her and accept her sisters. She needs a replacement husband."

The others mumbled in agreement.

David shook his head. "Where are we going to find a replacement husband this late in the year? Someone who would promise to take good care of her and help her raise her sisters and a baby? Someone we trust to do this?"

All eyes were back on him.

He swallowed.

Slow smiles crossed the ladies's faces. David felt trapped. Yet, at the same time he did have a big house, there would be plenty of room for her sisters and a newborn baby. He sighed. "I assume you are all looking at me for the same reason I'm thinking?"

Lily gave him a hug. "You're house is huge, cousin, plenty of room for a large family."

"I suppose you're right." The idea of having Holly by his side as his wife was appealing, even though he vowed never to marry again. He never spent much of his pay so he had some savings. It would be enough to take care of a family and he could find more work to provide for them.

"David, I think we're pressuring you. Think about it for awhile, but don't wait too long. Time is of the essence. I may have a solution to get the sisters here before they have to ride the Mercy Train." Mr. Martin took out his paper and made another note.

David stood. His mind made up, he made the announcement to the delight of everyone there. "I will do this, I'll marry her. On one condition, you don't let her know yet. Let's give Holly the best holiday surprise she's ever had. I believe she deserves this gift."

The ladies began to clap. "A secret wedding! Sounds delightful! David, how about at the Christmas Ball? We'll all help!"

He turned to Lily. "Would you mind? I know you've planned out your party to the tee. I wouldn't want to mess anything up."

Lily hugged him again. "Oh, David! I think a wedding at the Christmas Ball is perfect. We can change a few things and surprise her at the end. I'm so excited."

"We all have to promise to keep this a secret. Can you ladies do so?"

They all stared at David as if he were losing his mind. "The question is, can you?"

Mr. Martin stood. He helped his wife up and took her hand. "It looks like we are going to take a fast trip to New York City, young lady. We better turn in, the train leaves early in the morning."

David nodded. "I can keep quiet. I'll be happy to marry her." There, he said it in front of God and these eight ladies who were going to help him give the biggest surprise of Holly Bell's life.

Chapter 5

Holly slowly backed away from the staircase. She had been restless lying in bed, and thought maybe a light snack would help. Since she had spied some cookies earlier, it wasn't hard to get up and head towards the goodies. Cookies and hot chocolate were on her mind as she made her way along the hallway, smiling to herself at how much she enjoyed David's company this evening. She halted when she heard the voices coming from the small alcove at the bottom of the stairs. At first she didn't understand what they were saying, but the last words coming from David stopped her dead in her tracks.

"I'll be happy to marry her."

Who was he going to marry?

Giggles, laughs and hushed tones ensued.

No longer hungry, she turned to flee. It sounded like a private conversation, served her right to stand there and eavesdrop.

But, David!

Even thought she was forcing herself to marry Mr. Worthrop, there was this tiny shred of hope that perhaps she might be able to stay in Wichita Falls. The place was filled with so much neighbourly love and kindness she had always longed for. People smiled at her, they said hello and seemed to care. She had felt so cared for tonight by everyone, especially David. He had almost kissed her. Almost. She knew when it was time to get on that train, she would miss him most of all.

Holly backed away from the railing where she had stood listening to the words that struck at her heart. She prayed David would wait until she was gone before he married. Even though she was promised to someone else, it would hurt to see him marry someone else. Why did her heart ache so much?

His words kept her up most of the night. By morning, she was achy and miserable. It didn't matter what anyone said, she told everyone she wanted to stay in bed as she didn't feel good.

Lily came in, concern written all over her face. "Holly, do you want me to call Doc James? I'm sure he will come see you right away."

"I'm just not up to seeing anyone today." She didn't want to face David, not after what he said.

"Nurse Ellie is sure to stop by. Let her know if you are having any issues with the baby."

"The baby is fine, awfully busy. Maybe that's what is wrong. The baby seems to be moving around, maybe last night's activities were too much." She hated lying to her new friend but all Holly wanted to do was hide under the covers.

Lily stared at her. "Did you get rest?"

Holly shook her head. "Not much, I was tossing and turning most of the night."

Lily nodded. "I see. Well, rest today. I'll have others check on you. David is working in the ballroom today. Perhaps he can come sit with you at lunch, make sure you eat something."

Holly shook her head. "I'd rather not see anyone today. Do you mind letting everyone know I'd like to be by myself unless there is news from the telegraph office?"

Lily stared hard. "I doubt there will be any news from there. Are you sure you won't see anyone? I'm sure David won't mind having lunch with you?"

Holly didn't want to see David, it would be too difficult. "I'd rather be alone."

Lily left then, stepping out of the room as quietly as possible. Holly heard the click of the door knob and buried her face in the pillow. All she wanted to do was sleep and forget she had met one of the most loving and attentive men ever. It wouldn't matter, she was spoken for. By a man who still hadn't returned her telegram.

A tightness in her belly made her gasp. Holly took a few deep breaths until it was over, reminding her a baby would soon arrive.

Fear washed over her. She snuggled into the covers even more. She had taken care of her sisters for so long that she wasn't afraid to care for a newborn baby. But what if Mr. Worthrop didn't send her the money to buy a train ticket? What if he refused to collect her?

Being stuck here in Wichita Falls wouldn't be so bad except her sisters would be lost to her. She had promised them she'd come for them no matter what and was not about to go back on her word. If they stepped one foot on that Mercy Train, her family would be lost to her. She had to get a hold of Mr. Worthrop somehow. Another telegram would have to be sent but she gave all her money to David for the last one.

A few hours later a light knock at the door stirred Holly from her restless sleep. She opened her eyes, already knowing it was the one person she had wanted to avoid.

David peeked in the door, a grin on his face. "May I come in? I have some soup for you?"

The smell wafted into the room, making her nose twitch. It did smell awfully good. Her belly grumbled just then. Holly couldn't help but giggle when David made a funny face. It was no use, he was too charming to keep out. "Come in, then. I am hungry."

Holly sat up in bed, while David worked at settling the tray on her lap. Even though she hadn't wanted to see him today, the food he brought had changed her mind. She needed to feed the baby, keep herself strong and seeing him was a bonus.

"Thank you," she said in between bites. "I'm famished."

He pulled up a chair. "I know you wanted to be alone and rest but we are all concerned. As your friend, it's important you eat. What is the possibility of getting you outside this evening for another walk? I promise to make it shorter this time."

She shook her head. "I better stay here, resting. I've had some stomach pains and I'm not sure if it's the baby moving or getting ready to birth." Holly had no clue but she had to keep away from him. Too much time alone was not good, especially since he was bound to marry someone else. She wondered who it was? Maybe she should ask. After all, if they were friends then he would want her to know. "I hear that-"

A disturbance like no other was heard outside in the hall. It sounded like a hundred little feet were rushing along the corridor. Since David had left the door wide open, the noise got louder.

"The puppies!" David laughed. He scooped a few of the pups up and placed them on her bed. Little tails wagged like nobody's business. Two more fluff-balls ran along the coverlet, their tongues aiming for anything in sight to lick. When they found Holly's face, she collapsed with tears of laughter. Soon, all eight pups were on her, wiggling, their tiny little bodies jumping and bumping into each other.

Like a General looking for its soldiers, Millie rounded the corner and let out two distinct barks. They were deep and made each little head look up in surprise. Little tiny bodies all scattered, jumping from the bed to follow their mother out the door. It was the strangest thing ever.

A lady peeked around the corner of the open door. "I'm so sorry about the puppies. Hello, I'm Caroline. I live in Mill Ridge and am married to Doc Hart. We stayed overnight but I had no idea the pups got out the room when my husband went downstairs earlier. They sure are a handful. I'm hoping to find wonderful homes for each one of them on Christmas Eve at the Ball. Nice to meet you, I'll see you then." She waved and disappeared.

Holly looked at David with amusement. What had just happened?

He shook his head. "I'm sorry, Holly. I do see it's got you smiling though so I'm not sorry."

She tilted her head. "David, you always find a way to make me smile. I hope you make your new wife as happy and put a smile on her face, too."

His look of horror worried Holly. Now she'd have to admit she was eavesdropping last night. A long sigh filled the air. It was truth time. "Oh, David, I'm sorry. I was hungry last night and started to go downstairs for cookies when I overheard the last of the conversation at the bottom of the stairs. I apologize for being a busybody. I overheard you say you'll be happy to marry her. It sounds like you want to surprise this special person in your life, so I promise to keep it quiet. I won't tell a soul."

He didn't say a word. Was he angry? She kept on, trying to read him yet found it impossible. "I'm so sorry, I didn't mean to eavesdrop."

He shook his head. "I would appreciate if you didn't mention this to anyone."

She nodded with a heavy heart. "I promise. I won't mention this to anyone, but it sounds like Lily and some of the women already know."

"I had to tell someone to help with the surprise. I'm going to ask her to marry me at the Ball. If she agrees, we will have a wedding ceremony right then and there on Christmas eve."

Holly forced a smile, staring into the empty bowl. "Well then, I want to be the first one to congratulate you. Forgive me for taking up too much of your time with all of my problems and issues."

He shook his head. "Never, Holly. You've been a good friend as well. "I'm glad we met."

She didn't have to force a smile this time. "Truly, so am I. You've been wonderful to me."

He patted her hand. "Perhaps you can help me with some things."

Holly didn't want to help him with anything if it had to do with another woman. She wanted to pull the covers over her head and hide from the world. A sadness began to ascend through her whole body but she had to be polite. "What is it, what do you need help with?"

"Hmm, well, I am afraid I haven't bought a wedding ring for the bride, yet. I don't know what ladies of her caliber would like. I hate to ask you this, but would you mind taking a stroll to the merchants today and help me choose a ring for my bride?"

"I don't know, David, what you are asking is a strange request."

David's face fell. He must be in love with her. She had thought, well, no, impossible dreams had to be squelched! She had to shake these thoughts from her mind. His words had settled everything for her now. He was about to become someone else's husband. She was about to become someone else's wife. There was no more sense in wanting something that would never be. It was time for her to move on.

"I really want to make this so special for her. She deserves so much more." He even pouted when she looked at him.

Holly frowned. "Where is this lady, if I may ask? I haven't seen you with anyone, David."

David ran a hand over his brow. "She's away."

"Oh?"

He nodded as if the thought just struck. "Yes, she is in Dallas visiting her family and due back here Christmas Eve and that's how I can plan this all out without her knowing. She will be here on the last train."

Holly glared at him. "David! You tried to kiss me! How dare you while your future bride is away! How awful can you be to do something like this when you are in love with someone else! I can't believe you are in love with her and you tried to kiss me!" This was worse than terrible! Holly's throat tightened and her heart began to beat like a run-a-way mule team.

His jaw tightened. At first he reached out, then quickly drew back. David stood up, took a few paces back and forth then stood over her. "I guess the truth is I was missing her so much I got carried away with all the holiday celebrations. I didn't mean to cause you any harm. You are my friend and I took advantage. I'm sorry."

Holly was overwhelmed at the look on his face. He truly did see the error of his ways. "Promise me one thing, David, and I will go with you to help you pick out her ring."

He sat back down. "Anything."

She smiled. "David, promise me you will never again look at another woman. You must be strong and save it for your new bride."

Even though it hurt her, she had to tell him, to make sure he would never betray the woman he loved. Above all else, Holly valued her friendship with David more than anything. Her feelings for him were so strong. She truly wanted him to be happy.

He took her hand. "I promise never to even think about anyone else except the one who stole my heart." He raised dark lashes and looked deep into her eyes.

How was she ever going to forget this man? He stared at her as if the words he spoke were meant for her. The air was getting too warm.

"I think I need to rest now. I'll meet you this afternoon to look at rings for your beloved. I'm finished with the tray."

David was about to say something then picked up the tray and left.

After the door closed, Holly settled under the covers and let the tears fall. How did she fall for this man in such a short period of time? Yet, Holly knew exactly what had happened.

David was kind and caring with her best interests at heart. He would make a wonderful husband and father, except it wouldn't be to her. Yet, she valued their friendship and was determined to help him make his wedding day a wonderful memory.

Holly rose from her bed, unable to hide any longer. Her life here had only begun and was now ending abruptly. It was time to stand up and face the world. Pasting on a smile, she made her way to see Lily.

Chapter 6

By the time Holly went downstairs, the basket of puppies, along with Caroline and her husband were leaving through the front door.

"It was nice meeting you," Caroline called out over the whining and tiny barks coming from the basket. The puppies wanted out. Caroline struggled to keep pushing their little heads down while her husband tried to help.

"We really need to find them homes, my darling Caroline," Holly heard him say.

She waved, feeling slightly bemused and sad at the same time. Holly struggled with her emotions, which seemed to change day by day. She was afraid this baby inside of her was pulling the strings, causing her to be upset one moment and happy and content the next. Her moods were forever changing from one to the other. Yet, she longed for a relationship like the couple that just left. They seemed to fit perfectly. The same as Lily and her handsome husband, Ben. Those two were forever sneaking off somewhere, laughing and making eyes at each other. Everyone knew what they were up to and though it to be adorable.

As Holly walked towards the front desk, her thoughts on the people of Wichita Falls, she ran into a hard wall. Her hand went out to find David's chest. "I'm sorry David. I wasn't watching where I was going."

He grinned. "I can see you had your eyes on the little basket of pups. Maybe Santa will bring you one for Christmas."

She shook her head. "I would not know what to do with a little minx like that. They nip and bite and run all over the place. Besides, I'll have my hands full with a baby. And, my sisters," she added.

He nodded and held out his arm. "Are you ready to take a walk with me to the merchant?"

"Of course," she told him, even thought it was the last thing she wanted to do. Holly would rather he be buying the ring for her but that was impossible. He had already promised himself to someone else.

A sadness ripped through the air as they strolled along the boarded walk. Holly stared at his profile, trying to take it all in, to remember him when she began her new life in California. Which reminded her. "David?"

"Hmm." He seemed to be enjoying the stroll. A slight smile was on his face, and when he looked over at her, Holly noticed how happy he appeared.

She slowed down some, finding it difficult to bring up the dreaded subject. "I, um, hate to ask you but since we are friends, I'll hope you can listen in the spirit for which it is intended."

He stopped. "What can I do to help?"

"I am in need of a small loan to send another telegram and wonder if you may spare a few dollars until I can repay you."

He tilted his head. She worried he would look upon her as ungrateful for everything he had already done. She had never had to ask anyone for a favor like this before.

His hand went to her cheek. "Of course. Anything for you."

She wanted to step back and reprimand him for touching her but the warmth of his fingers made her lean in to them instead. She closed her eyes, enjoying the moment.

He chuckled softly. Holly's eyes widened when she realized how easily he had pulled her in. Heat swept across her cheeks. She turned away, embarrassed. "You did it again, David. How can you do this so easily?" Her heart hammered so loud she knew the saloon across the street must be able to hear the erratic beat.

"I can't help myself," he said, his tone so low she almost had to lean forward but caught herself.

"David! This can't go on. I can't be seen out in public with you if you are going to try these things. What will people think?"

His smile made Holly struggle even more. "I'm so sorry, it's just that I am so darn happy today."

How was she supposed to stay mad at him when he seemed so sincere? He may not even realize what he was doing. With one arm linked in his, she patted his sleeve with her other hand and sighed. "It's ok, I'm sure it has to be nerves. Don't worry, we'll get you fixed up with a ring for your true love and that will be one step closer for you." *And one step further away for me!*

The bell above the mercantile jingled when they entered. "What can I do for you folks?" The shop owner stood behind the counter, hands on hips, a smudged white apron hanging from his neck.

"Do you have any wedding rings, Mr. Wheeler?"

"Well, congratulations are in order first."

When David didn't correct the store owner, Holly felt the need to. "Oh, it's not for us, per say."

Mr. Wheeler squinted at the two of them. "No?"

She shook her head. "David's fiancé will be in on the last train Christmas Eve. He's going to propose. I'm here to help him choose a lovely ring." Her voice cracked when she spoke the words aloud.

David stared at her.

Mr. Wheeler began a coughing fit so loud he had to excuse himself to recover. He began to move around in the back room, knocking some boxes aside as he stumbled through the door.

"Is he all right?" Holly asked, puzzled at the old man's behavior.

"Seems fine to me," David told her. His face was a bit pale.

"Are you all right, David? You don't look well. What's going on here?"

David turned away. "I'm not sure I know what you mean. Look here, Holly. Here are the rings. Come take a look."

Moving over to the far counter, she dreaded picking out a ring for his bride to be. Why couldn't, no, forget that. This was serious business at hand. She had to give all her attention to this. David was her friend, she wanted him to be happy. "Which one do you want for your bride?"

He stared at the variety under the glass counter. "I'm not sure, I like them all." Without turning to look at her, David asked, "If you were getting married, which ring is the one you would choose to wear?"

Holly stood beside him, peering down at the exact one she'd want. She pointed to a beautiful gold band with a tiny diamond in the middle. Unable to speak for fear he'd hear her voice break, she nodded and tapped on the glass.

His brow rose when he finally did look over. "It's quite dainty."

She swallowed. "It's perfect," she whispered.

The smile he gave her made her heart almost stop. He seemed so gloriously happy she didn't want to end their experience on a sad note. Her heart may be devastated but Holly was not going to let him see.

"Mr. Wheeler! I've found the one!"

Jim Wheeler marched over, reaching in the glass case to pull the ring from its place. He handed it to David. "Take a good look before I ring it up." He snorted at his own joke!

Holly watched David as he placed the ring between two fingers. It looked so tiny Holly didn't realize she was holding her breath.

David handed it her way. "Do you mind trying it on? I think your fingers are pretty close in size to, uh, my bride to be?"

She nodded. He slid it on her left finger. Holly's heart was hammering so fast she feared it would pump all the blood right out of her. She knew the moment her eyes pooled with tears. They were about to spill over at any moment. "It fits. Here. I'm not feeling well all of a sudden. I'll wait outside."

She scurried down the aisle towards the front door, fiercely trying to keep the tears at bay. Fingers grasping at the door knob, she blindly twisted the it and let herself outside. The jingle of the bell rattled in her ears.

Fresh air, or as fresh as it could be in a small town like this one, filled her lungs. Holly grabbed a hold of the wooden rails on the porch, her knuckles white as she struggled to stay afloat. She almost laughed out loud. How could she go along with something like this! What a fool she was thinking it wouldn't have any affect on her.

In her state of mind, Holly knew it was best if she stayed hidden away in the hotel room until the baby was born and she was on her way to California.

"Holly, are you ill?" The jingle of the bell was almost too much for her tender ears.

"I'm fine," she snapped. Holly went to take a step away from the railing when she began to feel dizzy.

"I got you," David's sweet voice rendered in her ears. Before she knew what was what, he had her in his strong arms, marching across the street towards his cousin's hotel.

"Put me down," Holly mumbled, although she was feeling perfectly fine in his arms. Except people were staring at the two of them. "What will people think of me? Your bride will be here any day now."

"I don't much care what anyone thinks. Besides, everyone knows." His jaws snapped shut.

Holly was feeling ill but she didn't miss his last words. "Everyone knows what?"

David looked down at her, his dark eyes troubled. "Holly, no more talking. You overdid it today. It's best you rest. Just hang on to me."

It did feel good to have someone take over. She had always been the one to fix everything when it came to her life. Her sisters were always taken care of before her. Holly's husband, who was selfish, still received top notch treatment from her, although she hadn't known he was a horrible man until afterwards. She had adored her family and made sure they were always taken care of.

David seemed to want to take care of her. At least for the time being. She knew it would change when his bride returned. So, for this moment, Holly was ashamed to say she wanted to feel special.

Her body snuggled closer to his chest. As he walked down the street she closed her eyes, listening to his heartbeat against her ear. She didn't even bother to open them when he walked through the brightly lit lobby of the hotel and up the flight of steps. The weight of the mattress felt wonderful against her back.

She hadn't even realized what she said at first when he tucked the coverlet against her chin. "I love you."

Her hand was encased in his own warm one. His mouth brushed against her knuckles. "Holly." Her mind exhausted, she drifted off with the sound of her name on his lips.

"That was a close call."

"What made you think she wouldn't get upset? Holly is in love with you."

David smiled to himself. She had whispered her proclamation of love as she drifted off to sleep. He had wanted to wake her up and tell her that she would always be safe. Yet, the thought of a big surprise on Christmas eve was even more exciting. He could hold off a few more days. He had to. "I know what I'm doing, cousin Lily. Trust me."

She snickered. "I've never known to trust a man who uses those exact words."

David grinned. "I'm too darn happy right now to care what you or anyone thinks. I know you told me it may not be a good idea to play on her emotions but when she finds out the ring is for her, she will forgive me. I'm certain. When she sees the special gifts that will be here on Christmas Eve, she'll love me even more."

Lily shook her head. "David, are you certain?"

"About the special gifts? Yes, I got another telegram earlier from Mr. Martin."

"No, about the surprise wedding. Maybe it's too much for her."

"Miss Addie was right, you know. All she needed was a replacement husband. That's me. I can handle this."

Lily turned with a hand on her hip. She leaned down close to his face. "Let me tell you one thing, cousin David. If Holly gets upset at you, I can't say I blame her. It is one thing to become the replacement husband, but I'm not totally in agreement that you should wait to tell her until Christmas Eve. I'm having second thoughts on this big surprise. She still thinks that miner from California will send her a ticket. The no good louse, refusing to send more money and going back on his word. She has to be told sooner or later."

"Don't worry your heart out, Lily. She'll be more pleased at all the goings on here. She loves me."

Lily shook her head. "Has she told you she loves you?"

"Without realizing, yes." He wanted to keep it to himself, savor in the thought of her whispered words. David wanted Lily to stop pressuring him into telling Holly the truth. Everyone loved surprises, didn't they?

Lily sighed. It was one of those big, heavy sighs that made David realize his cousin wanted him to listen and pay attention. He found himself thinking of Holly so much lately, he had a hard time concentrating on what was at hand.

"David, I believed the surprise was a grand idea but now that you've told me how upset Holly was at the mercantile, I worry it may affect the baby. She's due any day now. Too much stress isn't good for a healthy delivery."

"Maybe I should talk to Nurse Ellie or the doc."

"I would. Yes, go talk to Nurse Ellie. If she thinks it will harm Holly or the baby by what you are doing, then you'll need to take their advice and it will take some pressure off of me, too. I certainly don't want anything to happen. I am concerned."

David grazed Lily's cheek with a quick kiss. "Thanks, cousin. You're right, I need to talk with the doctor. I don't want to cause her any harm or the precious child."

While David waited on the porch at Doc James's office, several townsfolk tipped their hats. "We can't wait to see the bride's surprised face," one of the others called out.

David stood up. "Now, will you hush! What if she were right here? How'd you find out anyway?"

"The whole town knows what you're doing. Why, before the decorating was over everyone knew. You can't keep a secret in a town like this!"

That was true for sure. David sat back down. He took his own hat off and wiped a hand over his brow. If everyone knew what he was doing, how was he going to keep it a surprise? This was hard work keeping a secret.

Nurse Ellie waved him inside. "How may we help you today, David?"

"I'm reluctant to discuss this but I figured you and the doc would know what to do."

Nurse Ellie smiled. "Well, you have quite the secret, David. I'm sure Holly will be ecstatic that you came to her rescue."

David sat down on the chair by the door. His head hurt. "I'm afraid the whole town knows except Holly."

"Well, of course they do. How else do you suppose to pull this off if no one knows? It takes a town to work together for such a surprise."

"I guess you're right. I am afraid when I took her to Wheeler's Mercantile to help me pick out a ring for the pretend bride, she was a tad upset."

Ellie sat down on the chair beside him. "You did what? James, come over here." She waved to her husband, who had been filling small bottles at his pharmaceutical cabinet.

He turned to stare at her, a pair of glasses half way down his nose. When she crossed her arms, he put down the bottles and pulled the glasses from his head. "This looks serious." He bent over his wife to kiss her forehead, resting a hand on her shoulder.

David didn't know what to say. "I am here to ask a question about Holly's health."

Doc James nodded. "Go on."

Nurse Ellie interrupted. "James, he took Holly to the mercantile to try on a ring, pretending it was for his bride that is coming in on the train Christmas Eve. Remember, I told you it was a farce, there is no bride except for Holly."

"Oh, for Pete sake, David!" Doc James grabbed his black medical bag. "I better go check on her."

"James, perhaps she should be resting in bed until Christmas Eve, don't you think so?"

James stopped. He nodded before rushing out the front door, flipping the closed sign. Groans from the front porch were heard inside. No one liked when the doc had an emergency call. It made their wait a lot longer, sometimes having to come back the next day.

David wasn't sure what had happened. "I didn't do anything wrong. Did I harm her baby?" He placed his head in his hands, leaning over, elbows on his knees. He had been selfish, thinking she would love a surprise when all along it did nothing but perhaps place the woman he loved in danger.

"Now, now, David. Doc James will check her and make sure she isn't too upset. I suggested bed rest so you can get done what you have to do. There will be no more tricking her though. Things like this are too stressful for a woman bearing a child."

"This is bad. I didn't think it would matter, now I see my error. I can't be a good husband this way. I'm calling the wedding off."

Nurse Ellie shook a finger at him. "David, calm yourself. You've already swore you would take care of Holly and the baby and her sisters. You can't go back on your word now!"

David stood up to look out the window. He paced back and forth, causing Nurse Ellie to tap her foot. He knew she was getting aggravated by him. "I'm sorry, you are right. I've taken this on and I'm going to see it through. I better go tell Holly the truth."

Nurse Ellie took a shawl from the hook beside the door. "David, come with me. Let's have some lunch at Jenna's Café. You need to eat and keep up your strength and I need to enlighten you on how it works in a woman's world."

David reluctantly followed Nurse Ellie out the door. It didn't matter what she said, he was going to be honest and tell Holly the truth. Even the truth about the heartless man in California who left her sitting high and dry.

Chapter 7

Holly was surprised to see Doc James. Usually, Nurse Ellie was the one to check up on her condition. "Good morning Miss Holly. May I come in?"

"Of course, Doc James. I didn't know it was time for a visit so soon."

He pulled up a chair and sat down. "It's not. Nurse Ellie will be along later in the week for your usual routine check up. I'm here because I heard there was an incident at the mercantile today."

"I got a little dizzy is all."

"You should not be getting dizzy. May I take a look?"

"Of course."

After the doctor's thorough examination, Holly was relieved to hear him say everything looked fine. "I suggest complete bed rest until Christmas Eve."

Holly stared at the doctor. "Why Christmas Eve?"

He coughed into his fist, turning his head but she didn't miss the worried look on his face.

"Is there something wrong, Doc James?"

He sat back down so his eyes were level with her own. "No, nothing at all. I tell all my patients the same thing. It's so close to your delivery that bed rest will help you at the birthing to deliver a fine, healthy child. You do want that, don't you?"

"Yes, of course I do. Okay, so bed rest it is. I won't get out of this bed until delivery."

Doc James scratched his chin. "I think it would be fine for you to go downstairs to get a little exercise though."

Holly was getting suspicious. For some reason Doc James was giving her conflicting orders. "Which is it, Doc, bed rest or exercise?"

He stood, snapping the black medical bag shut. "I think both. It is wise to stay in bed as much as possible except for meals, which you may go downstairs for. Also, to shower or bath and go to the privy. I don't want you outside or on a wild goose chase with David. The mercantile visit today was too much."

"Does the whole town know about my visit to the mercantile today?"

He nodded. "I'm afraid so. Nothing stays a secret in this town."

That was the answer she was hoping for. Holly smiled, promising the doctor she'd rest in bed. The moment he left, she flung the covers back. His last words made her smile. She was hoping nothing stayed a secret.

It was why she was going to find out what exactly was going on. Holly was suspicious there were shenanigans happening right in front of her. She wasn't sure of the reason but she knew it had to do with her. It was time to do a little investigating, after all, she had nothing better to do since she was ordered to be on complete bed rest.

A smile curved her lips. The doctor was fibbing. She was good at reading people and he had lied through his teeth. *Bed rest my foot!* Now that she had something to keep her mind occupied, she was starting to feel better, especially since she suspected this all pointed back to David. A clear picture began to form in her mind.

Making her way downstairs, she searched for her friend. Lily was in the library where she was delicately dusting some very old books, then placing them back on the counter. "Good morning, Lily."

Lily turned, her skirts swinging wide. "Why, good morning, my dear. Would you like to have some tea with me?"

"I'd love to." Holly settled herself on the settee while Lily brought a tray and set it down. She sat directly across from Holly. That was good, Holly thought, at least I can look into her eyes and see the truth or lies written there.

They chatted for quite some time while drinking the warm liquid. "Tell me, Lily, what is the hot topic in town these days?"

Lily eyed her from above the rim of the teacup. "Whatever do you mean?" The smile she gave Holly was extremely fake. She hated to question such a lovely person, but doing things behind her back was not very nice, even though she was sure David had planned some kind of surprise.

Holly leaned forward. "I believe there is a conspiracy going on and it has to do with me."

Lily batted her lashes. She looked towards the door to see if anyone was there. "Whatever do you mean?"

"I am sure David has asked you to remain quiet about the whole thing, hasn't he?"

Lily turned to the door again to make sure no one was listening. She leaned closer. "I'm so sorry, Holly. David is my cousin and I love him dearly but I told him not to keep things from you. Especially after the episode this morning. I don't wish any ill harm to come to you or the babe."

Holly smiled. Now she was getting somewhere. "How did David plan to pull this off? Who else knows?"

Lily laughed. "Why, the whole town knows. Everyone has been sworn to secrecy until Christmas Eve when it all comes to light right here on the ballroom floor. I'm sorry now that I may have ruined the surprise but you already had suspicions about this."

"Indeed, I did. It started at the mercantile when David asked me to try on a ring for his betrothed. I have to say I was extremely upset when I learned he was going to be married. David doesn't really have a betrothed, does he?"

Lily reached over and patted Holly's hand. "He does not. I'm sure you were upset about it, dear. But now it's all out in the open and you can relax some. There's nothing else you need to do now. No worries. You will be taken care of. Please, don't tell anyone you know and act surprised. He's working so hard to plan this out."

"How did he know I was listening at the top of the stairs?"

Lily shrugged. "I don't know the answer to that."

Holly stood. "Thank you for the tea but there is so much you don't understand."

Lily stood. She reached for Holly's hand again. "It's all in place. The wedding ceremony. The ring that you already tried on. All you need to do is be here for the ceremony. Everyone has been secretly getting ready for this. Please, don't worry."

Holly held back tears. She placed a hand over her heart, which was heavier now than ever before. "I know David told me the telegram never came. But it did come, and their plans to have Mr. Worthrop surprise me on Christmas Eve is a grand gesture. Except for one tiny detail." A sob caught in her throat.

The look of shock on Lily's face that she guessed what all the ruckus was about made Holly feel even worse.

"Holly, I don't know what to say," Lily stuttered, taking a step closer.

"You don't have to say anything. I didn't plan to fall in love with David."

"Oh, dear Lord!" Lily gathered Holly in her arms. Tears fell like nobody's business.

Holly cried so hard she barely remembered Lily helping her back to bed. "I'm sorry for the tears, Lily. I wish I had a choice. I love it here in Wichita Falls."

Lily paced the room. She turned to Holly. "You get some rest. When you wake up, your head will be a lot clearer. Right now, I'm going to go clear up some things with my cousin."

Holly was bewildered at Lily's words. It was true, she wished she didn't have to marry Mr. Worthrop but her sisters all deserved a good home with someone to care for them, not a children's home or Mercy train where they'd be separated.

Her mind was exhausted. A tiny twinge clutched at her belly. The little one was getting louder each day. Taking deep breaths, Holly knew she had to stay calm. It wouldn't do any good to get upset. What's done was done. In a few days, she'd be Mrs. Guy Worthrop. On one hand, it made her happy to know she was able to provide a home for her wayward sisters. On the other hand, well, she just wanted to throw up.

<> <>

"David. She thinks you and Mr. Worthrop are in cahoots!"

He sat down, placing his head in his hands. "Oh no! This is turning into a total mess!"

"Perhaps its time you told her the truth. I know you wanted her to be surprised but she's upstairs crying her eyes out."

"She is? I should go to her." David rose, ready to take the steps two at a time to be with Holly.

Lily blocked his path. "No! You sit there and listen to me! Now, David!"

The fire in his cousin's eyes was flashing like mad. He sat down. "We are going to pull this off. I get it, I want her to be so surprised and with the Martin's secret trip to New York, her Christmas eve will be the best she's ever had." Lily peered into his eyes. She was stubborn and he sat there paying attention. Lily was no one to trifle with.

David nodded. He grimaced. "I should go to her."

"No. You stay away. From now until Christmas Eve, I don't want to see you near her room, do you understand me, David Morgan? As a matter of fact, you are fired!"

He stood. "What? Why?"

She giggled. "Don't look so horrified! I don't want you near this hotel until then. You are too vulnerable. Go to your shop and work from there. I'll send over what I need for you. David, you can't pull this off, your emotions are too unstable. Now that you know she thinks Worthrop is the one marrying her, I can see it in your eyes you'll spill the beans."

"I can keep quiet."

Lily crossed her arms. "I highly doubt it, David. You are lovestruck. Now that Doc James checked to make sure her and the baby are fine, we have a lot to get ready for. Christmas Eve is in two days. Have you heard from the Martins yet?"

He nodded. "Mister Martin sent a telegram yesterday. They will be here around six Christmas Eve as long as everything goes smoothly."

Lily nodded. "Good. Now you go on. I don't want to see you here until then."

"I really want to see her, make sure she is fine."

Lily pushed him towards the front door. "Go, David. She is resting. If you come near the hotel, you will ruin everything."

Seven women, several babies and two toddlers walked through the front door together to help with last minute preparations. David watched as they all disappeared into Lily's office.

He stood alone in the foyer. David thought maybe he might go upstairs to peek in her room, make sure she was truly okay.

"David, good-bye!"

Lily's voice echoed through the large foyer. "Good-bye, David," was repeated seven more times.

"All right, I'm going!" Slamming the door, he sighed. How was he going to stay away for two more days?

"Why the frown?" Sheriff Montana asked. He slowed when he saw David.

"Am I frowning? Didn't realize I was."

"Don't let him back in here for two days, Sheriff, else he'll ruin the surprise!" Lily slammed the front door.

David grunted. "My own cousin throwing me out of the hotel until Christmas Eve."

The sheriff laughed. "Why's that, son?"

He shrugged. "She thinks I'll ruin Holly's surprise."

Sheriff Montana grinned. "Why don't you walk along with me to Dawson's place. Play some cards."

David looked back at the hotel. "I guess I can. Nothing but time on my hands now."

Sheriff Montana shook his head. "I guess you best come along, then. Get your mind off the lady."

David fell in step with the Sheriff. "I suppose. It's complicated. She thinks that lying, heartless Worthrop is coming to town to marry her. Except he sent a telegram stating he was no longer interested since she was broke."

"Figures. Some of them miner's find a wealthy woman and use all their brides money on the mines. I'd say it's a blessing she wasn't able to get there."

"A blessing for me, too, Sheriff."

Sheriff Montana nodded at the others sitting on the porch. "Hey, fellows. David here needs to take his mind off his upcoming nuptials. What say we play some cards?"

A few men sat around a small table on the front porch of the Land Title office. David recognized all of them. He shook hands with Marshall Montgomery, who had a ranch outside of town. He was Ruby's husband. "Marshall."

Dawson Sloan, Grace's husband nodded while the owner of the newspaper, Daniel Ashwood scribbled in a small notebook. He stuffed it in his front pocket, along with a pencil. "Good day, David. Guess my wife and the rest of the ladies are hard at work finishing up the last minute preparations for the party?"

"It looks that way," David mumbled.

Sheriff Montana swung his leg around one of the empty chairs. "He got kicked out of the hotel. Lily was worried he'd ruin the wedding surprise."

The others chuckled. "Don't you worry none," Lily's husband, Ben, told him. "The ladies will give you and Holly a wedding like this town has never seen before."

"Lily won't let me see Holly after her fiasco at the mercantile. I just wanted to make sure she's all right."

A black buggy slowed in front of the house. Max Ward, one of the richest ranchers in the whole area jumped down, greeting the others.

The others shook hands and laughed. "You and that fancy, shiny buggy!" Dawson teased.

"I only buy the finest to escort my wife in. I just dropped her off at the hotel to help the ladies. Guess all you men are here for the same reason. They all at the hotel?"

"Yep. Sure are. You may as well get settled here and play some cards. Looks like it's going to be a long day."

"Fine by me," Max told them. "Got most things wrapped up for the season. Now it's time to enjoy the fruits of my labor."

Dawson looked at David. "What he means is throw his riches around us poor folk."

"I mean no such thing," Max joked.

"You two knock it off!" Sheriff Montana's voice was not too serious. "Max has done more for this town than anyone else besides Miss Addie. Speaking of our honorable matron, here she comes."

The older woman was holding a parasol in one hand while smiling and waving to others on the street. She turned to the men. "Good morning, gentlemen. I feel the holiday spirit in the air. David, chin up, this too shall pass," she told him, crossing the street towards the hotel.

Everyone looked at David and laughed. Max Ward shook his head.

"Is it that obvious?" David asked the others. He pulled some bills from his pocket.

"Yep."

"Sure is," Dawson grunted. He dealt the men some cards. "What charitable event are we playing for this time?"

Max Ward began to deal the cards. "The school's almost built. We still need to hire a school marm. Let's raise money for her salary."

David laughed and shook his head while picking up the cards in front of him. "I heard through the grapevine you men play cards once a week while the ladies get together. Didn't know you play for charity though."

Ben nodded. "Yup. There's always someone who needs a bit of help. We've taken the winnings and bought a weeks worth of groceries for one family down by the river last week."

Daniel spoke up. "It makes for a great story on the front page. Especially when everyone knows Max Ward can give to charities with just the interest he earns at the bank."

Max flipped his hand over. "Two pairs. Now gentlemen, it's easy to just give money away, but this here, I look forward to spending time with you boys every week."

"Here. Here."

The glasses of ginger ale went up in the air for a toast. No one drank liquor because of Dawson's prior problem with alcohol. David was glad to be a part of the community, a part of their group. "Thank you for inviting me," David told them.

"Son, you'll find out our brides, our work and family take up much of our time and we don't mind that one bit. It's what a man does. But, now and again, men need time to sit and talk with like-minded souls. We've found a way to give back to Wichita Falls and have this at the same time."

The sheriff raised his glass again.

"Pretty clever," David said, raising his own with the rest of theirs. He gazed at the hotel. "Do you think everything is under control?"

"Shut up, David. Our women know how to take care of things. Let's play cards."

Chapter 8

Christmas Eve 6:15 p.m.

David stood at the rail road station, his hands deep in his pockets. The train was late! Sweat formed at his brow. This was not good! He made his way to the ticket booth, knocking on the window for the forth time in the last ten minutes.

Charles looked at him, frowning. He marched over, slid open the window, and stuck his head through. "David, for crying out loud! I can't get my work done if you keep pestering me! The train is always late. Always! Now don't bother me again!" He slammed the door shut then opened it about three inches. "Merry Christmas to you! I'll see you at the party!"

At half past six, the ticket master flipped the sign on the window to closed. Since there would be no more trains for the next twenty-four hours, Charles didn't have to wait on this one. That left David alone on the platform, wondering what was taking so long.

What if the train robbers stopped the train again? They hadn't been caught during the last episode. What then? Everything would be ruined. He paced back and forth wearing the wood platform thin, worrying about things that were mostly likely never to happen twice in a row.

A hard object deep in his pocket reminded him not to worry. Before the night was over, Holly would be his wife.

Wait until she found out everything was not as it appeared to be. He had been faithful to his word and had stayed away from the hotel for the last two days. It had been hard but the men kept him so busy the time flew by. Before he knew it, his feet were planted right here, on the rickety train platform waiting for Holly's biggest surprise of all.

This was a good town. He turned away from the tracks he had been staring at for the last five minutes to gaze upon main street. Tales had been told about Wichita Falls younger days when unruly men wandered the street. It had been so dangerous, Miss Addie's own sister had left town to never return again. He had heard the town grew by leaps and bounds over the years, bringing more decent folk thanks to Miss Addie's matchmaking skills. She had brought the kind of women here that were able to tame the frontier men.

Most of the homes along the main street were dark, along with the businesses that had closed early to attend the enormous Christmas Ball. He watched in amusement as the ladies covered their faces with a half-mask.

He grunted. He recognized almost every single person who wore a mask. Miss Addie for one, she was on the arm of Maximilian, ranch foreman to the Montgomery Ranch. She wore a red velvet gown that trailed behind her. A white shawl covered her shoulders, along with the red mask. He would know her anywhere and so would all of the townsfolk.

A low whistle sounded in the night sky from a few miles away. David sighed, relaxing his shoulders. He hadn't realized how nervous he had been. This was it. The train was coming and in a few minutes he would be on his way to marry the woman he loved.

The clip-clop of horse's hooves echoed through the empty streets. David turned to watch two wagons stop in front of the hotel. Lily had out done herself, hiring the boys at the livery to stand in front of the hotel in red jackets with gold trim and hats. Each buggy that had arrived would be taken to the livery to be parked while the horses were watered and fed.

Two more employees stood at the front door, wearing an immaculate long-tailed black tuxedo to escort each person into the ballroom. Lily and Ben opened up the whole hotel so no one had to leave, offering a room for those who had to travel. The residents of Mill Ridge had been invited along with many farmers and ranchers in the area.

The tracks shook as the train got closer. David's pulse beat erratically. He stuffed his hands in his pockets as deep as they would go. A small crowd from somewhere along the main street was singing Jingle Bells, their voices fading as the sound of the train coming to a stop overpowered any other noise.

The train came to a dead stop.

Mr. and Mrs. Martin were the first to get off the train. Dressed in bright red and white Santa outfits, they looked adorable. It was a nice touch for what was about to happen.

David smiled. He was about to get married and give his wife to be one of the greatest gifts ever.

Chapter 9

Holly let the tears fall. There was no stopping them now. Even though it was supposed to be the happiest day of her life, the dread of marrying someone she didn't care for or even know hit from out of nowhere.

The women were helping her get ready. Lily had loaned her a beautiful pale yellow gown while Ruby hand stitched a beautiful new lace veil that trailed down her back. Hannah was fixing her hair, sweeping it up on her head, while letting some tendrils curl around her face.

"This is something blue," Grace said, placing a lovely necklace with blue tinted gemstones.

"Thank you," she said before bursting into tears.

Holly tried to cover her face but Rebecca knelt down in front of her, holding her hands. "It's okay to cry. But, don't worry. Everything will work out accordingly. I promise."

She closed her eyes. "I know," she whispered. "I'm sorry, guess it is bridal nerves."

Sophie gave her a hug. "I brought a pair of my Sunday shoes for you to wear. I believe we are the same size." Holly slid them on her feet, standing up, taking some deep breaths while facing the seven women who helped her get through the last few days.

Ellie handed her a handkerchief. "Now, Holly, if you feel any discomfort, please let one of us know right away. Today is your due date for delivery. Let's hope the little one holds off until after you are married."

"Thank you, each and every one of you. I've never felt so loved in all my life. I wish I was able to stay here in Wichita Falls. In this short time, I've made many wonderful friends."

Sophie spoke up. "Well, I don't loan my shoes to just anyone."

The others laughed.

Holly was close to tears again. "This is for the best. Marrying Mr. Worthrop will enable my sisters and I to be a family again."

Ruby patted her hand. "You never know. Sometimes miracles happen."

Holly shook her head. "I've learned it doesn't happen to me." Holly took in a deep breath. She nodded to the ladies. "I'm ready. I heard the train whistle blow so my intended must be here. Do I look like a bride?"

"A beautiful bride."

Holly gave them all a hug. "Thanks for keeping everything hush, hush. Where's my mask?"

Ellie handed her the half-mask. "Boy, won't David be surprised when he sees you."

Holly's heart was in her throat. David was bringing Mr. Worthrop to surprise her at the Ball. The girls came up with the idea to dress her as a bride so when Mr. Worthrop did surprise her, she'd already have a wedding gown attire on and they could be married right away.

Then she didn't have to hurt anyone's feeling because she already knew. "David will probably appreciate you ladies helped him without realizing it." Her voice shook when she said David's name. How was she going to be able to get on a train to California with her new husband and never see him again?

Because she had to. There was no choice. Her sisters were her responsibility.

One of Lily's employees stuck their head in the room. She didn't say a word but disappeared the moment Lily spotted her. "Shall we go to the ball?" Lily announced. "Ladies, how about we make a grand entrance like no one has ever seen before?"

All seven women descended down the wide staircase. Holly thought it odd when the carolers voices stopped out of the blue. Most of the crowd was gathered in the large lobby, their voices whispering. Holly wasn't able to see over the top of the other women who had made it a point to go down the stairs first. Ellie had stayed by her side in case she had any difficulty.

The front door swung open. Holly heard more whispering, then some giggles from the rear of the crowd.

"What's going on? I can't see anything."

Ellie didn't say a word. The other ladies ignored her, too.

Something wasn't adding up. Where was Mr. Worthrop? A fear almost as disheartening as when she faced that awful train robber clutched at her heart. Holly clutched her hands together as she stood at the bottom of the stairs. Had he not been on the train? Is this what all the hush, hush was about? "Someone please tell me what's going on?"

Giggles erupted from the rear of the crowd again. They almost sounded like-" Holly stepped forward. She knew the sound of that laughter like the back of her hand. She pushed the other ladies aside and they moved out of her way making a path right through the crowd.

She was almost afraid to call their names. It was them, it had to be. No other giggles were quite like her sisters. "Polly? Molly? Jenny? Julie?"

The crowd parted rather quickly as four young ladies erupted in loud, shrill laughter. "Surprise!" they all sang in unison.

Tears streamed down Holly's face. Her sisters jumped up and down and gave hugs and kisses while Holly tried to hug back. Except her belly was in the way. After some time, the crowd clapped, and she remembered the whole town was there, watching. Which was kind of weird, she thought. But then Wichita Falls was not like any other town she knew.

"Perhaps being married to him won't be too bad after all." She didn't realize she had spoken out loud. "Where is Mr. Worthrop?"

The crowd got quiet again. Holly looked around for her groom but the only other person she noticed was David. Oh, David! Why couldn't it be you? She closed her eyes, agony and defeat clouding over her. This was supposed to be her wedding day.

She accomplished what she had set out to do. Her sisters were here, in her arms, safe. What a nice feeling to have them here. She smiled at David. "Thank you for the surprise. Now, where is Mr. Worthrop? I want to get married and take my sisters home." *To California, so far away. Too far away from you! Oh, how will I ever be able to leave here?*

David moved through the crowd to stand in front of her. His smile ate at her very soul. She was so incredibly happy and yet horribly sad at the turn of events.

She gave him a sad smile. If she was to leave here a married woman, she wanted to remember David smiling at her. She wanted their last words to be a wonderful memory she could hold in her heart and keep to herself forever.

He stared into her eyes. Holly held her breath. "I'm afraid I have some bad news. Guy Worthrop won't be arriving."

Holly looked at him. He didn't seem upset. She gazed at the crowd. Every single woman was watching them, wide eyes and some with their mouths open as if in anticipation. As if they were waiting for something to happen. The men, their brows were raised, some bored, some not showing any emotion at all.

She whispered. "David, what is going on?"

David took a step back. Oh, God, where was he going? Instead of turning away, he went down on one knee.

"The ring," Sheriff Montana urged.

Holly froze. "David Morgan, you set me up?"

The smile on his face belied how nervous he was. Holly realized when she saw him swallow. He reached in his pocket and cleared his throat. "Holly?"

She raised a hand to her throat, fingering the necklace there. "Yes," she whispered. Her sisters gathered closer.

"I'm sorry I lied to you. I wanted this to be a big surprise so I let you believe Worthrop was coming here. Thanks to the Martins, they were able to get your sisters in time. As for me, I don't want much except for you to be my wife."

The tears ran down her face. She took a step towards him, nodding her head. "Oh, David. I. No! Oh!"

Pain shot through her, tightening her belly like never before. Her sisters grabbed her arms from both sides. David looked devastated at first. "No? You won't marry me?" His voice was low, his tone devastated while the crowd began to murmur.

She shook her head. "No, I mean, yes, I will. Oh, the baby!"

The instant he realized she was about to give birth, David got up and scooped her in his arms, taking the stairs two at a time. "Get the doc!"

"We're having a baby!" someone shouted from the crowd.

"The baby's coming!"

"What? Holly's giving birth! How wonderful!"

Holly heard the shouting from afar. Her heart was so happy. She wanted to jump for joy at David's proposal. Too bad it was interrupted. "I'm sorry," she told him, cupping his cheek with her hand. "I'm sure you didn't plan on this happening."

David placed a kiss on her forehead. "We will be married before the night is over."

"We will?" Another contraction hit hard. Holly gritted her teeth. She wanted to push the baby out right now!

"Yes."

"Can you please take care of my sisters while I, while I give birth?"

"Yes." David tucked the cover around her while Ellie and Sophie followed them into the room.

Soon, all seven ladies were there, shooing David out.

Three hours later David was pacing back and forth in the lobby. The crowd had thinned out some since most townsfolk went back to their homes. The others who had come from out of town and were staying at the hotel waited with David, patting his shoulder on occasion as he waited and waited for word from upstairs.

Lily's surprise was her husband's aunt, a famous singer who entertained the crowd. When she was done singing for the evening, she came over and gave David a kiss on the cheek. "Congratulations," she said before her entourage led her upstairs like she was a royal queen.

The four sisters sat in a circle on the floor playing with the last puppy. Most of the other puppies had found good homes tonight. David had watched Caroline's husband, Doctor Hart, set the basket of puppies down as they sniffed and jumped and carried on until they found the person they decided to keep.

Elizabeth and Grant from Mill Ridge took one puppy, while Sophie's husband Salem already had one picked out. Or, the puppy picked him out because as soon as they were freed from the basket, the pure black one went right to Salem. He scooped it up and carried it around all night.

The only one left was now in the hands of Holly's sisters. They were laughing and giggling so hard it made him smile, distracting him from the activity upstairs.

Lily's husband, Ben smiled at the sisters. "Guess you not only have a new family, but a pup as well." The girls giggled and gave the pup even more hugs.

"I wonder what's taking so long?" David asked, distracted.

The moment he asked, Lily appeared at the top of the stairs. "David, you can come up. Holly wants you to bring the Reverend."

Reverend Connors heard his name. He followed David up the stairs, bible in hand. Mrs. Connors wasn't far behind.

David took a long, deep breath before entering the room. The baby wasn't his but he imagined it was. Holly was propped up in bed, a clean gown covering her. She smiled at him, her eyes glistening. A tiny bundle was in her arms, resting against her bosom.

David stood over her, placing a kiss on her brow. He looked down to see the little bundle. The baby was beautiful. "There are no words to describe this moment."

"Meet our son, David."

His eyes met hers. "That means the world to me," he told her, placing another kiss on her cheek. "Can we get married right now?" he whispered in her ear. "I brought the reverend."

Giggles were heard from the door. David looked back to see all four sisters peeking around the corner. "Come in, girls. Take a look at your nephew."

Jenny was holding the puppy when it jumped from her arms onto the coverlet. The puppy bounced over the bed, scooting close to the baby. It sniffed the blanket he was wrapped in then plopped down and snuggled close as if it was where it belonged, his little eyelids closing.

Everyone in the room laughed.

Reverend Connors cleared his throat. "Let's get this show on the road. Who wants to get married this evening?"

David and Holly gazed into each other's eyes. "We do," they both said, echoed by four giggling girls and a sleepy puppy's incredibly loud yawn.

*****

Thank you for reading Christmas in Wichita Falls. This feel good story is one of my favorites and I hope you enjoyed visiting with the gang in Wichita Falls.

Can you keep a secret? Or, should I say can three men, the sons of Nora White keep a secret? They have a secret they've kept from their mother for almost ten years. Now grown, Nora wants them to marry. She knows they'll never have a life of their own if she doesn't do something about it herself. So, she meets with renowned matchmaker Miss Addie and proceeds to find some good Christian women for her sons, starting with Luke, her first born.

Here's a little piece of A Bride for Luke:

Chapter 1

Prologue 1870's

Nora White stood in front of the boarding house on Main Street in Wichita Falls ready to make a deal with the devil. Well, perhaps not the devil. She heard many great things about the matchmaker Miss Addie. She wouldn't be here if she had heard any different. It didn't help her nerves were all over the place.

"Only the best for my sons," she whispered. Her voice caught the wind as a man walked by, tipping the rim of his hat in greeting. "Good day to you, ma'am."

Nora tucked back strands of dark lustrous hair peppered with gray. If there was one thing her husband always said it was she had a great head of hair. A slight smile curved her lips at the nostalgic thought. She still missed Robert so much. He had always taken the time after a long day to place a hand over her cheek and tell her how beautiful she was. He had done it every single day no matter how exhausted he was after a hard day's work on the ranch they owned.

Enough day dreaming, it never got her anywhere. Squaring her shoulders, she stood in front of the big door and lifted a hand to knock.

Before she made contact, the door swung open. A beautiful woman stood there, one of advancing age but well groomed with dark hair and wearing a lovely, expensive gown. "Welcome to Wichita Falls, Mrs. White. Please, do come in."

She held the door open while Nora contemplated spinning around and walking away.

It wouldn't get her sons a good wife if she did so.

Miss Addie led her to the dining room table, offering her a seat while picking up a tray from the side board. "Let's have some tea," she offered, setting a cup in front of Nora.

"Thank you, Miss Addie. I'll get straight to the point. I hear you are the best match-maker in the whole of Texas and beyond. Is this true? I want only the best for my boys."

Miss Addie smiled. "I suppose you are referring to my one hundred percent success rate? You've come to the right place, my dear. Now, what is it you want me to do for you?"

Nora sighed. This Miss Addie was certainly sure of herself. When the decision came upon her to find her sons good Christian women, the others in church told her of Miss Addie's success. She had immediately sent a letter not expecting a reply so fast. Within two weeks, the woman had replied with an appointment to come see her. Two hours later, she found herself smack dab in the middle of the Main Street of Wichita Falls. "I've heard this town is mostly filled with mail-order brides that you are responsible for?"

"You heard correctly. I've chosen the best grooms for the lovely ladies and the most suitable women. This is my life, Miss White. I don't mess around or truffle with tender feelings. You may expect the best, top-notch service from me."

"Thank you."

"Now, tell me about you?"

"Me? Why me? I have no interest in a man? I want this for my three sons."

Miss Addie leaned forward, setting her tea cup on the saucer with a delicate hand. "Miss White, in order for me to find your sons a good, Christian wife, which is what I believe you said, I'll need to know all about the woman who raised them. Fair enough?"

Nora nodded. "I suppose." She didn't like to get personal with others but this was for a good reason. Her sons were her world, her life.

"Tell me about you, Miss White."

"First of all, please, call me Nora. I've been a widow for ten long years now. The boys lost their father and I lost a good, hard-working husband when rustlers tried to steal some of our cattle. He was wounded by one of them and never recovered."

Miss Addie steepled her hands. "I'm sorry for your loss. What is it that brought you to me, Nora?"

"I'm getting older. From the day my husband died, the boys have taken over the ranch. When I tell one of them to go find a nice, sweet Christian woman, they shrug it off, determined to be there for me. I'm not going to be here forever, Miss Addie. I want them each to have a full life with a wonderful woman and not take care of an old lady, but they won't try to find their own happy life."

"You are hardly old, Nora. Why, there are plenty of eligible men who would agree with me."

A blush spread across her cheeks. It had been a long, long time since someone said such a nice thing. "I'm obliged to your kindness, but it's my sons I'm concerned about. Can you help them?"

The noise of a teacup being set on its plate was the only sound in the room right before Miss Addie pushed her chair back. "Of course, I can help. Now, let's take a walk to the porch out front while you tell me who is going to be the first to marry."

Standing on the porch, Nora felt so relieved. Instinct told her she must trust Miss Addie to find the best wife for her oldest son. He was the one she worried about the most. "May as well start with

Luke, my oldest. He's been taking care of everyone and everything since Robert's death. Luke is quiet, yet dignified and he is angry."

"Angry? Will this be a potential problem for a bride?"

Nora shook her head. "No, I don't mean he is mean or would hurt anyone. He is so serious all the time. In my heart I'm sure he is angry at his father for leaving us and yet Robert had no control of fate. But he will take care of his bride like he has taken care of the ranch and his brothers. He gives his heart and soul to those he loves. He has a fierce loyalty to all of us."

Miss Addie nodded. "Perhaps he needs a bride who will be willing to show him some kindness. Let me think on this. I'll be in touch."

<><>

A week and a half later a letter arrived. Nora slipped off to her bedroom to read what Miss Addie sent:

Dear Nora,

I do believe I've found the perfect bride for your son, Luke. She has a situation and needs to leave her home town immediately, thus, this letter of urgency sent to you today. It isn't drastic but a choice of hers where she does not wish to marry an ageing friend of the family. I have further investigated and am reassured Miss Abigail Wheatland is all she claims to be.

I've sent her the details and a ticket to arrive in two weeks time. Therefore, you will have the same amount of time to inform your son of his impending marriage. Enclosed, please find a photo of Miss Abigail Wheatland and some other facts about the nuptials. I would have liked to meet your son and spend time with him, which is what I normally do in cases like this. However, since you and I have already met, I've determined you are an honest and upstanding citizen so the need to meet with your son will not take place.

Please inform him of the details of our conversation. Miss Wheatland will arrive expecting to be married immediately. I will expect him to be at the Wichita Falls train station on the sixth of September to fetch her and bring her to the church for the official ceremony.

Yours truly,

Miss Addie

Nora stared at the letter. She thought there would be more time to prepare her son of the upcoming ceremony. Now, she'd have to do it and soon.

Yet, a week and a half later, she was still contemplating what to do. Nora saddled one of the horses. She needed to think. Riding was always her way to explore the vast land her husband had purchased so long ago. The green hills, valleys and pastures where their cattle grazed made her feel so alive, as if there were no cares in the world. Nora may be ageing but with years in the saddle, she could ride like nobody's business.

Hours later, after refreshing herself with a long jaunt, she slid from the mare, walked her and brushed Fancy Lady down. She smiled at the name for the honey-colored horse. Whenever the mare left the barn, she'd walk as if she was the fanciest girl in town, lifting her tail up in the air along with perking her ears and raising her front feet higher than normal. It always made Nora laugh.

"Glad to see you're smiling," her oldest remarked. He came around the side of the large barn, his tall form intimidating to many except for his mama.

She gave him a look of consternation. "What's that supposed to mean, young man?"

Luke sighed. "Young man? I'm barely young, Mama. Twenty-seven is not young."

Nora grinned. "You are still the most handsome of the boys, you know that, right?"

He rolled his eyes. "Yes, and the most fun, the most original, the best at wrangling cattle and your favorite. You say it to each one of us. At any time any one of us can suddenly become the favorite."

Nora laughed out loud. "You boys are on to me!"

He actually smiled, showing a set of white teeth. "We've known all along."

Nora's way was teasing all three of her boys so they always thought they were the most important. Yet, each one knew how much they were loved in their own right. Her boys were her life but she didn't want them to make her theirs.

They all needed a bride.

It was now or never.

She led Fancy Lady to the coral to graze. After returning to the barn where Luke was brushing down his own horse, she placed a hand over his. "We must talk."

Luke raised an eyebrow, but immediately stopped what he was doing. "What is it? Is something wrong?" Luke stood, throwing the brush on a bale of hay then thrusting his hands deep in the pockets of his pants.

"Maybe we should sit down to talk," Nora warned.

Luke leaned back on his heels. "Let's get this over with right here, Ma. You are looking too serious to waste time finding a seat."

"You are a smart man."

"I'm my mother's son if it is any reassurance." He smiled again, the love for his mother shining in dark eyes.

Nora noticed how handsome he was, how much he looked like her Robert and told him so. "You have your father's smile."

Luke's eyes darkened. He grinded his teeth and frowned. Nora never understood why he seemed to be angry whenever she spoke of Robert. But now was not the time to find out, she had more important things to deal with.

Nora walked to him, taking his hand in her own. She cocked her head and looked at her oldest son, proud of the man he had become. "I know you don't like when I talk of your father and I'm not sure why. Perhaps you are still angry at him for leaving us. It's been ten long years, Luke. It's time to move on. It's time to take the bull by its horns and start new lives."

His eyes widened. "What? Are you trying to tell me you are marrying someone else? I didn't even know you were courting anyone. How did I miss this? Ma, what is this about?"

"There will be a marriage."

"What!"

"But it won't be me."

"What do you mean? What in tar-nation are you trying to tell me then?"

Nora sighed. Her eldest son was so dramatic. He was an angry man, filled with discontentment and yet was the most loyal and trusting one out of all her sons. She imagined Robert would have been so proud of his oldest son. "I've determined none of my boys will ever leave here to try to find a life outside of this ranch. Or," she held up her hand, seeing his mouth start to open wide, "bring a bride here to make a life as I have."

Luke stared. He shook his head. "I don't care about making any other life. I'm perfectly happy right where I am."

"Let me finish. Ranching is a hard, lonely life. When the day is finally over and all the work is done, what do you do?"

He shrugged. "I don't know, either take up with Sam or Adam and play cards with the other hands on the ranch. What does it matter?"

"Luke, you haven't experienced true love. Sitting on the porch, having a glass of lemonade with the person that means the most to you will bring out the best in you. Imagine a walk at night watching the stars, working hard all day to be able to give your wife a kiss when you get home. There's so much more to this life than you are experiencing."

"I don't care about those things."

"You don't because you haven't experienced them. Luke, I've taken matters in to my own hands."

He turned. "Ma, what did you do?"

She nodded, determined to make him understand. "I've sent for a mail-order bride for you, Luke. Please, before you refuse, just please give it a chance."

"No."

"It's too late, she is already on her way here."

He shoved his fists deeper in his pockets. She almost smiled at the way some things never changed. He'd been doing that since he was five years old and found out he had pockets in the britches he wore.

"What? You can't order a mail-order bride and not even ask me! Besides, what kind of woman would do such a thing as come out to the West not knowing what she was getting?"

He pulled his hands out and then they went back in his pockets. Soon, he'd balance himself on his heels.

"A woman who is forced to marry an old man three times her age by parents who only want the money the marriage promises, that's who. There are even worse stories I'm told."

She actually noticed a worried look cross his face. Her son actually had some emotion when it came to other people besides his own family. What a nice surprise to realize. She'd have to play on that, even though it wasn't nice to do so. But he wasn't giving her much choice. His refusal was expected but this was harder than she had thought.

Was she doing the exact same thing his bride's family was doing? Forcing a marriage on two people who didn't want to be married? Biting the side of her bottom lip, Nora was determined to see her sons happy and they would never do this on their own. She had to help them. It was a whole different situation than the brides.

"The contract from the match-making agency is clear. You must marry immediately upon meeting, however, if, after three months, you both wish to part ways, there will be an annulment granted as long as the marriage bed is still pure."

"No."

"Didn't you hear what I said?"

"The answer is still no."

She wasn't going to drag him to the alter. He had to at least want a small part of this. What was she able to dangle in front of him to convince him to give it a try?

"I'll give your father's pistol to you if you agree to try this for three months."

"Agree."

"I know it's not exactly what you, what did you say?"

"Agree. I've wanted that pistol every since Samuel said he was going to claim it last year."

Nora blinked. "You would marry this bride so you can get one up on your brother?"

Luke nodded. "Kind of looks that way, huh?"

Nora threw her hands up in the air. "Oh, for Pete's sake! If that's all I had to do, well, then when it comes time to have the talk with your brothers, tell me what they want?"

Luke backed up, his hands out in front of him. "Now, Ma, do not make me tell my brother's secrets."

Nora smiled. She knew Luke would tell her. If he had to get married, he'd make darn sure it was going to happen to his brothers as well. "It's a yes, then?"

"Of course."

She placed her hands on her hips, a smile from ear to ear. "Well then, be ready to pick up your new bride at eight-thirty Saturday morning at the train station in Wichita Falls."

"So soon?"

"I'm afraid so. Now, what is it the other boys want most of all?"

Luke shook his head. "I'll tell you when the time is right." He straightened up, a serious look on his face. "Ma, even though I'm getting married, you will always be my favorite girl."

A tear slipped down Nora's cheek. Her first born would always be special, too. Instead of telling him that, she wrapped her arms around his neck and gave him a big old hug. "I love you, son. You know I'm doing this for you. All I want is for you to be happy."

"I know, Ma."

A Bride for Luke: Book 1 [1](https://www.amazon.com/gp/product/B079FLSKV7)

Sons of Nora White is [2](https://www.amazon.com/gp/product/B079FLSKV7)

---

1. https://www.amazon.com/gp/product/B079FLSKV7

2. https://www.amazon.com/gp/product/B079FLSKV7

AVAILABLE NOW![3] (https://www.amazon.com/gp/product/B079FLSKV7)

---

3. https://www.amazon.com/gp/product/B079FLSKV7

To get on Cyndi's Exclusive Mailing List, go to Cyndiraye.com and pick up a free copy of Miss Addie: The Beginning. It is the story of Miss Addie and how the Wichita Fall Mail Order Matchmaking began! Only exclusive for Cyndi's readers. It will never be published on any book site.

Get Miss [4]Addie[5]'s story here FREE[6] (http://cyndiraye.com)

---

4. http://cyndiraye.com

5. http://cyndiraye.com

6. http://cyndiraye.com

Cyndi's Other Books

Mail Order Brides of Wichita Falls Series
Ruby
Grace
Lily
Charity
Hannah
Rebecca
Sophie
Ellie
Jenna
Leila
Boxed Set Vol 1-8
Boxed Set Vol 9-12
Christmas in Wichita Falls Holiday Book
Brides of Mill Ridge Series
An Outlaws Honor
A Reverend's Rose
The Ranger's Redemption
A Doctor's Devotion
A Teacher's Treasure
A Sister's Sanctuary
Sons of Nora White Series
A Bride for Luke
A Bride for Adam
A Bride for Samuel
A Groom for Nora

A Bride for Russell

A Bride for Wesley

A Groom for Widow Young

Multi-Author Series Contributions

A Bride for Abel - The Proxy Brides Book #4

A Bride for Calvin - The Proxy Brides

A Tin Star for Christmas - The Belles of Wyoming

Candy Cane Christmas - Ornamental Matchmaker Book #10

All these books and more can be found by visiting

https://www.amazon.com/Cyndi-Raye/e/

B00ENA1WEG

****

If you haven't read the Brides of Wichita Falls yet, get the first 8 books in one boxed set

Mail Order Brides of Wichita Falls Boxed Set[1] (http://amzn.to/2yeRaIP)

---

1. http://amzn.to/2yeRaIP

Don't miss out!

Visit the website below and you can sign up to receive emails whenever Cyndi Raye publishes a new book. There's no charge and no obligation.

https://books2read.com/r/B-A-PXQ-XMMFC

Connecting independent readers to independent writers.